Lady Georgiana Chatterton

Country Coteries

Vol. 2

Lady Georgiana Chatterton

Country Coteries
Vol. 2

ISBN/EAN: 9783337427511

Printed in Europe, USA, Canada, Australia, Japan

Cover: Foto ©Andreas Hilbeck / pixelio.de

More available books at **www.hansebooks.com**

COUNTRY COTERIES.

BY

GEORGIANA LADY CHATTERTON.

IN THREE VOLUMES.

VOL. II.

LONDON:
HURST AND BLACKETT, PUBLISHERS.
13, GREAT MARLBOROUGH STREET.
1868.

LONDON:
PRINTED BY MACDONALD AND TUGWELL,
BLENHEIM HOUSE.

COUNTRY COTERIES.

CHAPTER I.

A Secret Expedition.

ON the morrow everything seemed to favour the secresy of the expedition; for Lady Lillyford said at breakfast that she had promised to drive out Mrs. Winchfield, and call with her at a few places.

"And I shall get a list of men from her—all the best—Well, never mind, I shall not want you, so you may finish your letter to your grandmother, and explain how it is I have no time to write to her."

Beatrice was greatly relieved at the proposal, and determined to lose no time in writing the letter, that it might be ready for post, in case Miss Gubbings should detain her longer than she expected in the City.

Lady Lillyford started very punctually, for in spite of that little Mrs. Winchfield's propensity to flirt, Lady Lillyford always enjoyed a talk with her, for she knew more what was going on in the world than any-body, and she had the agreeable knack of amusing even the " stupid Lady Lillyford," whom Lady Horatia declared she " could neither amuse nor offend."

Beatrice ran upstairs to put on her bonnet the moment she heard the carriage drive off —for she was afraid that visitors might call, or some untoward interruption occur. Then, taking her grandmother's letter downstairs to the post-box, aud the key of the Square from the dining-room, she glided out, and arrived at the appointed spot. She had not long to wait, for Miss Gubbings soon ap-peared at the corner of the Square, and came quickly over the crossing to the gate with her veil down, and an old shabby shawl thrown over her dress, so that no one at a little distance could have recognized the fashionable Miss Gubbings, who was said to spend half her income on her dress.

" Come quick," she said, " or somebody will see us from the windows, and be sure to wonder and tattle."

They found the cab waiting half-way down the next street, and succeeded in reaching it, as they thought, unobserved.

" Now drive on quickly," she said to the cabman, " and you shall be well paid."

Miss Clementina Gubbings, or, as we shall henceforth call her, " Clemmy," expressed her gratitude so warmly, that Beatrice could not help being glad that she was able to give so much pleasure. Moreover, as she had often felt very curious to see the Miss Gubbingses' mother, and so find out the real cause which prevented them from living with her, she began to tremble less at the secret expedition.

During the drive Clemmy confided more

fully to her the conflicting feelings about Roland which had caused so much sorrow for the last two years, and how difficult had been her position with her sister.

"Meely," she said, "is so very touchy and jealous if I am admired or loved more than she is, and, in fact, never rests till she has succeeded in estranging from me anyone who takes a fancy to me. She even tells them I have less fortune than she has, and that she alone will inherit our mother's part."

"But are you sure that you like Roland better than any other person?" inquired Beatrice, who, divining, from Clemmy's description of her sister's jealousy, that she had often admirers whom she did not wish, or, at any rate, had not wished to discard, began to think that Clementina's love for Roland could not be very deep.

"Oh! yes, indeed I do. It is very foolish, I know, when I might do so very much better; but I can't help it—indeed I can't,

so pray do help me!" Then she spoke of
her mother with great affection, and said
that nothing could make her so happy as to
be with her and see her often. " For really
I should never feel ashamed of her, as Meely
does," added she; " except perhaps just in a
certain set. But I do love her, poor dear,
very much; and I know she so bitterly re-
proaches herself for having tried to make
such fine ladies of us. Of course she had
no idea we should be so ungrateful (that is,
Meely) as to desert her and be ashamed of
her. Since I have loved Roland so dearly,
and suffered so much myself, I have begun
to feel for poor ma's disappointment about
us. I do, indeed; and I feel for her still
more since I knew you, and see how beautifully you bear with your mother, who is
very aggravating often, I know, only in a
different kind of way; and she is not half
so good as our Ma. Oh! dear Beatrice, I
often think if there is a Heaven, that Ma
will be so much happier there than any of

us, though she does wear an old hair front and ugly dress, and leaves out all her h's, where they ought to go in. I know you would love her in spite of it all; and I know she'd dress better, and become any-thing, and would be ever so much nicer, if she thought anybody cared for her. But she is broken-hearted at times, I fear, and moans after poor Pa."

"And has she really no one with her to take an interest and——"

"Only old Sooky, our nurse, and she has such a bad temper, that I know she leads Ma a sad life; though she's very fond of her too. But she can scarcely read, for her eyes are bad, and she never cared much to read either, so she must be dreadfully dull."

"Would she not be much happier in the country?" asked Beatrice. "Surely the birds and flowers and trees would give her great pleasure? Do you know, I never knew before what it was to feel real enjoy-ment—to be happy in every-day common life, until I went to dear old Oakhampton. Why could she not · live in some pretty country place ?—she can afford it."

" Oh! yes; but she will *not* leave the old house, I know. She goes and sits every day in the room where papa died, and kisses the chair where he used to sit."

As they proceeded along the dull and narrow streets that led to that part of the smoky city, Beatrice felt more and more compassion for the poor woman who seemed to sentence herself to banishment from all the beautiful sights and sounds of this fair world, and thought how miserable must be the state of mind which thus rejects all con-solation.

" It's because she feels her children do not care for her, I suppose," said Beatrice, after a few minutes' silence.

" Yes, I know it, and feel we are very guilty—very; and I indeed think it's a punishment to me to be so wretched about Roland, and to suffer so from my love to him. It all goes wrong with me, and so it will with Meely—only much worse, I'm sure. But, then, she will never love any one as I do, so she will never feel so unhappy, perhaps."

"But she will suffer far more some day, I'm sure; and it will be still worse, the later it comes, for you feel it already, and that shows you are in a better state of mind, I know."

CHAPTER II.

The Button-maker's Widow.

" HERE we are. I told him the wrong number purposely—for caution's sake I wished to walk up to the door," said Clemmy, as they stopped at a door in a narrow dark street. Clemmy paid the man liberally, and waited to see him safely turn the corner; and when he was out of sight they proceeded to her mother's house. It was small and dingy, and looked as if the windows had not been cleaned for years. The knocker was so stiff, that Clemmy had difficulty in lifting it.

For some time the door was not opened. At last they heard a drawing back of bolts and bars, and a tall old maid-servant made her appearance, looking very cross and grumbling in a low tone at the number of stairs.

"Lawk! Miss Clemmy," she said, "is that you? Well, to be sure! I suppose it's some of them letters you are expecting of? But there ain't none this time. No—and so you are going to see mammy, are you? Stay and tell me, who is this young lady?"

"She is Miss Lillyford; you know whose sister, now," said Clemmy in a whisper. "How is my mother to-day? Well, perhaps I had better go in alone first; but no, I had rather she should see her before she knows who she is. So come, darling Beatrice, don't mind, only just look kind, and as you used to some of the poor people at Oakhampton. I used quite to envy them being looked at and spoken to as you did, I know it made them so happy—and so it will poor mammy, I know." So saying, she opened the door of a small back drawing-room, and Beatrice saw an old woman sitting in a corner, and looking so miserable, that even her daughter's approach did not seem to produce much effect.

"Dear mammy," said Clemmy, "I've brought this dear friend of mine to see you; and I know you will like her so much. She is so good and kind."

"A friend of yours who is good and kind? Well, Clemmy, that's something quite new, it is. It's the first time I ever 'eard o' sich a thing. Well, let's have a look at your face —don't be afeared, I'm not a-going to hurt you, though I be a rough old 'ooman out of the parish, and took out o' the workus, I was, by Jemmy; and I never thought to come a-nigh sich a lady as I see you be. Yes, you be a real lady, that I knows well enough to see; sich a one as no daughters o' mine 'ill ever be, for all the hedication they got, and the book larning. Well, well—and now they don't care what becomes o' their mammy, that they don't."

"Yes, indeed, Clemmy does," said Beatrice, as she looked into the old woman's face with her soft, loving eyes. "She told me so as we came along, and she wished she could make you happy, she did indeed."

"Ah! I can't believe that; though, since she loved a worthless young chap, I know she's softened like, a bit, she is. But it's a bad business. I fear she'll never be happy with him or without him; and to think it was for this my poor dear man toiled and moiled, up early and late to bed, and ate the bread of carefulness, 'a did. And I were more foolish nor 'e were. I know, and thought it would be a grand thing to have our childring made ladies of—more fool I."

"But, mammy, you never asked me who this beautiful lady is, who came all the way here in a common cab to see you."

"Well, if I hear her name what wiser would I be? I see plain enough she be good and kind, that she be; no need to tell I that. And I thank her kindly for coming to see me, a rumateck old body, in this 'ere dark old place. But how comes it you were not ashamed to bring her?"

" Because, dear, dear ma——"

" Call me mammy, then——"

" Darling mammy, because she is *his* sister."

"Oh! Miss Lillyford is it? Well, to be sure. Well, miss, what do you say to all your brother's doings? How he made up to my daughter—and took up with another grand lady, and then comes back to my daughter. What do you say to all this?"

"I can make no excuse for him at all," said Beatrice. "I fear—and—but Clemmy loves him in spite of it all, and perhaps if they were married he might grow better."

"Oh! I know he would!" said Clemmy.

"Never you mind—let the pretty lady speak for herself. Perhaps you bean't sure? I see that on your beautiful face, which can't tell no lies, if you wished it ever so much. I see that as plain as a piked staff—I does."

"But poor Roland has had great disadvantages, my grandmother says. She is very good, and knows and sees into people's feelings very often, and she sometimes tries to make excuses for him. You see we lived abroad for so many years, and he had no home in England—we were always going from one place to another, and he got so unsettled in his habits, and——"

"And your grandmother is a real good woman, then, be she? What, some'at like yourself?"

"Oh! much better than I am," said Beatrice, with a smile. "I'm only a young inexperienced girl—and I, too, have had great disadvantages—I know. I'm not at all clever —and—and I'm sure I am not good—but if you could see grandmamma, and two friends of mine—I am not to be compared with them, and they say, too, that Roland has had a very bad chance, and that they scarcely wonder he went so wrong."

"Is he fond of you, then, dear miss?

Then, tell me, 'as he any 'art at all—'as he the sense to see what you be?"

" He likes me better than he does most people, I think—yes, he is very good to me always."

" Well, and would you like him to marry my daughter?"

" I should indeed—I think it would save him, if she really loves him, and—and cannot be happy without him."

The old woman looked at her kindly— seemed to ponder deeply, then said,

" Well, miss, I'll think it over for some days. I don't go for to say but that I be more inclined to look favourable on him since I heard he was your brother. But I must think a bit—I must."

" But, mammy, you will give the thousand pounds to-day, to save him from arrest, won't you?"

" No, not now. Come here to-morrow, or the day after, and maybe I will, and maybe I won't. And, miss, thankee kindly for coming to this poor place; will you please to take some'at?"

"Nothing, thank you, dear Mrs. Gubbings. But we ought to return home; for no one knew I was coming, and they may wonder what has become of me."

"Oh! so you comed unbeknown to your fayther and mother, did you? Poor young lady, deary me, she don't look like one as could deceive—sure 'twill make her very unhappy—it's a shame for you to draw her into such a scrape. And was it because you cared for that ungrateful hussy of a daughter of mine, that you came, or for the sake of your brother, tell me, now?"

"For both—really I feel for Clemmy, because I see she is very unhappy—and poor Roland, I should like to help him if I could, very much indeed."

"Oh! you would, would you? Then he must have some good in him, I think. Well, I won't keep ye; for I see you be in a fidget to be home, and no wonder—for I know she's not given to deceiving, and don't like it. Good-bye, miss; let me kiss your pretty hand. Not a word more, Clemmy. You come back alone to-morrow, and I'll tell you then what I'll do."

Clemmy saw her mother was resolved not to commit herself; so, although much disappointed, she made the best of it, and, kissing her mother with more than usual affection, hastened downstairs.

They nearly tumbled over Sukey, who was so close to the door when they opened it, that Clemmy said,

"Of course you've been listening to all we said—you always do. Don't you now, Sukey?"

"And who's a better right, I should like to know, than the old nurse that reared you? And bad is the look-out for you to go and marry a good-for-nothing man, who'll most likely clean out your purse, and then leave you to be sorry for what you've done. Marry in haste and repent at last. Yet I

am not going to say but what I'd rather see
you take up with anybody instead of having
your heart frozen up into stone along with
your sister. It wad do ye good to work for
your own bread some day, it would."

This was said as they were going downstairs; and when she opened the hall-door
for them, and saw no carriage, she shook
her head, and said,

"You hain't a-going to walk all the way,
I know, like common Christians. The carriage is waiting somewhere round the corner, I suppose, 'cause yer afraid the fine servants should wonder and laugh at your own
old mother's house. Good day, miss—and
I wish you as much happiness as your pretty
kind face deserves."

This was addressed to Beatrice, who took
her rough hand in hers as she wished her
good-bye.

Clemmy hurried her away, for she said
they might have some distance to walk before they could find a cab.

CHAPTER III.

They meet with Untoward Adventures on their way back from the City.

"YOU have put them both in wonderful good humour, dear Beatrice," said Clemmy, as they walked along. "What a bright idea that was of mine to bring you here! Ah! there's a cab. Ho! stop!"

It was empty, but the driver did not seem at first to hear the call; and Beatrice began to fear, from the look of him, that he was not quite sober.

At last Clemmy succeeded in arresting his attention. He jumped down from his box, opened the door, and growled out:

"Where to ?"

"Set us down in Manchester Square—corner of Duke Street," said Clemmy.

"All right," said he, and off they drove at a furious pace.

"Are you sure he is sober ?" inquired Beatrice with some alarm.

"Not at all sure ; but I daresay he will drive us safe enough."

"But see how he turns the corners! Oh! do let us stop him !" said Beatrice—"do let us get out !"

It was too late, for in turning into one of the narrow streets he drove so furiously against a post that one of the wheels became entangled ; the horse plunged, the man was thrown off, and the cab upset. A crowd collected in less than a minute, and Beatrice, who was partly stunned by the fall, found herself lifted out of the cab by a tall dark man, who gazed on her with a look of insolent admiration that made her tremble even more.

"Thank you—I am not hurt; pray put me down. I can walk quite well," she said. "Oh! Clemmy, where are you?—who is this?"

"Don't be frightened, dear," said Clemmy, "for if you are really not hurt, there is nothing to dread. This is Sir Bevan Desborough, who most fortunately saw the accident; and as his carriage is here, he will most kindly take us home."

A well-appointed carriage and horses stood near, and although Beatrice felt a most unaccountable dislike to Sir Bevan, she thought it would be foolish to make any objection, so the footman let down the steps and they got in.

Clemmy sat next to her, and Sir Bevan opposite, gazing on her with the same kind of insolent admiration, and expressing earnest hopes that she would not suffer from her fright.

There was something so strangely repugnant to her in his appearance, manner, and the tone of his voice, and it all reminded her so painfully of the gaming-table at Baden, which she had sometimes seen when a child, and where she had seen her brother in later years lose more than he could afford, that, to escape the obnoxious glances of his eyes, she looked out of window.

She afterwards remembered that Clemmy put down her veil, and sat quite back in the corner of the carriage, as if to avoid observation, and that she herself ought to have done the same; but she became so bewildered with her previous fright, and present antipathy to their companion, that she involuntarily put her head almost out of the window, as if to escape from the bad atmosphere of that evil man.

"I knew your mother very well some years ago, Miss Lillyford, and very pretty she was—but your face surpasses hers; and, by-the-by, I must have seen your lovely self too, when you were a child in the Villa Reale Garden at Naples. Ah! you don't remember me, I see, so I must be re-introduced."

Clemmy whispered something in his ear, and then he continued to say—

"Oh! ho! I understand, a little expedition on the sly—never fear, I can keep a secret, Miss Gubbings—you well know that —not a word. And if I meet Miss Lillyford, as I devoutly hope I shall, at some parties or balls, I shall look as innocent as a lamb, and declare that I have the greatest pleasure in making her acquaintance then for the first time."

Beatrice trembled more and more at the further prospect of deceit; and particularly objected to have such a companion as that in her secret. She was going to remonstrate, but was interrupted by Clemmy, who pinched her arm and said,

"Oh! yes; for really it is of vital importance that our—that my visit to the City to-day should not be known, therefore I shall be most grateful to you if you will keep our meeting secret. And, Beatrice, dear, do put down your veil, and don't stare out of window in that way."

The caution came too late, for at that moment Beatrice saw a figure walking along the pavement that made her cheeks tingle, and, as the story-books say, her heart stand still.

" It must be !—oh ! it is he !" passed her lips ; but the next moment she turned deadly pale, for she saw that the joyous expression on Arthur Brookfield's face had changed in a moment on seeing Sir Bevan Desborough.

Sir Bevan, of course, turned round to see what object had caused that sudden blush and joyful look, and then he caught sight of Arthur Brookfield, whom he had not seen for three or four years. Now, if there was a person in the world he detested more than another, it was Arthur Brookfield. But he did not betray any surprise. He leaned indolently back in the carriage, watching

Arthur's receding form, and as he noted well the surprise and alarm depicted on the young man's face on seeing Beatrice in his carriage, a triumphant sneer distorted features which were often considered handsome.

Beatrice was too much horrified and perplexed at the sudden change on Arthur's face, to see or think of anything else.

"Oh! why was he not glad to see me? Why did he not stop the carriage?" were questions she continually asked herself, as they drove towards home, and pondered anxiously on the reasons which could have caused that sudden change of countenance, and the cold stiff bow with which he turned away and walked on. She scarcely heard anything they said during the remainder of her drive, but she afterwards felt that Clemmy and Sir Bevan had been talking of her.

As they approached Manchester Square he addressed a few courteous words to Beatrice, and expressed his hopes that he might soon have the pleasure of meeting her again.

It seemed as if her manner had gradually inspired him with a little more respect.

"Command me," he said, as the carriage stopped, "in anything, and at any time."

"Thank you," said Beatrice, with a decision which almost surprised herself. "But I hope I shall soon have no further cause for concealment."

Beatrice got out, put down her veil, and walked home so fast that she had crossed Manchester Square, and turned into Lower Berkeley Street, before Clemmy came up to her.

"Oh! Clementina, it was cruel of you to make me get into that man's carriage. I know it was wrong. I am sure that man has done something dreadful—something that makes all good people dislike him. Now, has not he? Tell me the truth."

"His character is not very good, I must confess; but he is very rich, and goes into the best society—he does, indeed, you will see he does."

This was a painful look-out for Beatrice, who said she hoped she might not be forced into any society where such men were tolerated.

"He is now an excellent *parti*," said Clemmy; "for his wife died last year, and he has got all her fortune, which is very large."

Clemmy did not add the current report that his heartless ill-treatment was supposed to have broken her heart, and that his wife's relations had endeavoured to dispute the will, for everyone felt convinced that poor Lady Desborough would not have left all her fortune, which was in her own power, to him, unless some cruel coercion or villainy had been practised. By this time they had reached Portman Square.

"Here we are," said Clemmy. "You had better go into the Square, instead of round by the pavement." Beatrice unlocked the iron gate and went in. "Now, cheer up, darling Beatrice," said Clemmy, as they parted, " and don't look so miserable, pray. I cannot imagine why you should be so cast down. There is really nothing to fear for *you*. You know it is *my* business that requires so much secresy, lest it should come to Lady Horatia's ears, for she is still so infatuated about poor Roland."

" Then how will she take it when it is known ?" Beatrice was about to ask ; but Clemmy made her a sign to hide under the trees, while she herself hastened away, enveloped in the shabby shawl, and limping awkwardly along, so that Beatrice in her innocence thought she had become suddenly lame.   But, as Clemmy afterwards explained to her,

" It was the better to disguise my usually springy and graceful walk, in case any people I knew chanced to see me cross the road."

CHAPTER IV.

In addition to her own Perplexities, Beatrice
hears Bad News about her Brother.

SHE soon disappeared round the corner,
and Beatrice was left alone with the
most painful of the perplexing thoughts that
had yet been forced into her mind. That Arthur Brookfield had returned home safe was
certainly a great relief; but why, having
returned home, why had he not called?
" This might have been the very day of his
arrival," she thought in his excuse, and he
had seemed for a moment glad to see her:
" yes, he had,"and again her eyes lighted and
her cheeks glowed with delight at the
thought.

" But—that might have been only surprise, and—he may have seen some one else all this time that he likes better. No doubt he has—and then—though he may like me as a friend, perhaps, it may suddenly have occurred to him that I might be disappointed when I heard that he is—perhaps married." And the poor girl endeavoured, with great courage and resignation, to realize the possibilities or probabilities of this startling fact—till the tears began to run down her cheek; but she soon brushed them away, and thought—

"Well, I never could be worthy of him."

Altogether her thoughts were so painful that she felt it necessary to take refuge in something else, or she would never be able to conceal her grief.

"And they will wonder what's the matter with me," she murmured half aloud.

Then the important question occurred to her, whether she should tell her mother that she had seen Arthur Brookfield, or not?

Oh! yes, was her first impression, till

she remembered that she would not be able to account for having seen him in the City, when it was not to be known that she was there herself at all.

No—she must not tell; and, after all, it would make but little difference, for if he cared for her still, he would certainly call or write. He would find out where they were, for their names were put down in the Court Guide. "Yes," she said to herself, "he will be sure to call, if—if he is not already married." This idea must be kept back, or her eyes would get so red. Then she anxiously looked up to the windows of their house, fearing that her mother might have returned, and would wonder where she was. There was, however, no signs of her having come back—yet it must be getting late, so she resolved to go home at once, and face the servants and her mother, without allowing herself any more time for thinking or crying.

So she crossed over, knocked at the door,

and was much pleased to find that her mother had not yet come home; and she hoped she should have time to bathe her eyes, and try to look more composed, before Lady Lillyford should return.

"He has found someone better or prettier, I daresay," she thought to herself, as she looked at her face in the glass, to see if her eyes were less red. And yet she could not help seeing that she was beautiful—not less, but more beautiful than when Arthur Brookfield saw her last.

"I do look better now," she said, half aloud, "for my eyes have more expression, I know, and my mouth does not look so silly as it used to look sometimes."

Then as the thought occurred to her that it was very vain and conceited to admire herself thus, she ran down stairs to the drawing-room, and began to read a novel which had interested her the day before. But although she had left off at a most critical part of the story, she found it now impossible to fix her attention, or care whether the heroine were extricated or not from her perilous position.

From this state of painful effort she was at last aroused by hearing her father's voice calling out with unusual impatience,

"Beatrice, girl, what are you at there? Won't you hear me? I've been calling to you all over the house. And where's your mamma?"

"I suppose she has not returned from her drive—she said she should be late."

"Why, it's near seven o'clock! I wish she had come in."

"Could I help, dear papa?" said Beatrice, fancying that her father seemed unhappy and agitated.

"Yes, darling, I daresay you could help, if you knew how—much better than any of us, and I am sure we all want help. Well, I may as well tell you, for it's sure to be known soon. There, Roland has been arrested at last, in spite of all we could do.

I do think, however, it's the best thing that could happen to him, if it were not for the disgrace. But I don't like the look of being here all so grand ourselves, and going to give balls and parties, while his tradespeople are kept out of their money; and there's no end of bills coming in to me—in hopes I should pay, but I really can't."

"Oh! papa, how I wish we had never come to town! I can't think what pleasure there is in those crowded parties, and driving about those ugly streets all the morning. Oh! I was so very happy at dear Oakhampton!"

"Yes, I know, darling—I thought so too; but, you see, we never somehow can have our own way; your mother does make such a fuss if she hasn't just what she fancies. I spoilt her at first, I know, for she was very beautiful, and I loved her very much. I never could be firm, and that has spoilt her. But I ought not to talk in that kind of way."

" I don't think that she really enjoys London either," said Beatrice. " I'm sure, if she would see something of the neighbours, and the dear Somertons at Oakhampton, she would not find it dull. And there are such very nice people now living at Ferncote. I saw them at Mrs. Dashville's ball —such a pretty girl, with an elder sister, and she was dancing with the Marquis of Somebody—I think it was the very person mamma was so disappointed at not being introduced to at Mr. Holloway's ball."

" I daresay; I always heard theirs was a very good family, and very popular. But it's of no use. Now, look here, dear girl, just help me to cast up these bills, and see what they amount to; they are some of the most pressing, I believe—at least, Henderson, the steward, you know, who has been here lately, says so. You are a good accountant, I think ?"

Beatrice took them at once, and, roused from her own grief by her father's real distress, she found less difficulty in fixing her attention than she had on the interesting novel. Sir Charles threw himself into an arm-chair, and took up the paper with a wearied look.

CHAPTER V.

*" To taking out Clementina, and putting in
Horatia, £2. 12s."*

MEANWHILE Beatrice proceeded with
her task in silence. There was an item
in one of the bills which caused her much
annoyance, but she did not deem it prudent
to mention it yet to her father.

It was from a fancy stationer, where Roland had bought some months back a very
costly and handsome album. One of the
extra costs of the album was for engraving,
in gilded and embossed letters, with an or-
namental border, the word "Clementina"—
£2. 15s. But what was her dismay and
surprise when, after a few other items of a

later date she read, "To taking out Clementina and inserting Horatia in the same beautifully embossed style."

Soon afterwards Lady Lillyford returned home, and on being informed by Sir Charles of the sad truth that Roland, her favourite and first-born, was actually in prison, she went off into hysterics, and they had great difficulty in pacifying her.

"Where is he?" she cried; "I will go there at once. Oh! Charles, how can you be so unfeeling?—why did you let this happen?"

"Because you ran me in debt yourself. You would take this house. I raised all the money I could borrow for him, and——"

"Oh! I'll give up anything to free Roland! Oh! do liberate him—take my jewels—take my rings!" said Lady Lillyford again bursting into tears and sobbing hysterically.

Beatrice was puzzled what to do; she thought it might now be expedient to tell her father about Clemmy, but felt she must not do so without her consent.

"Could she go and see her?" she asked herself; but no, she would write and tell her of the catastrophe without saying any words that Miss Meely Gubbings might not see.

So she sat down at once, and when she had written the note, directed one of the servants to take it before dinner.

For some time Lady Lillyford kept on exclaiming that she would go and see her darling son in prison—that she would start at once by rail—for he had been taken to the county town in D——shire.

Sir Charles for once very wisely made no opposition, for he felt sure that, at all events, she would want her dinner first, as she must have come home hungry after her long drive; and then, as it was a very cold night, she would probably wait until the next morning.

She, however, ordered her maid to pack

up her things, and kept up unceasing lamentations whenever the servants were out of the room.

Meanwhile Beatrice anxiously expected the answer to the note, in hopes that this crisis of affairs might induce Clemmy to confess to her sister the unshaken attachment she professed to feel for Roland, and that between them perhaps they might manage to extricate him from his painful position. But, alas! no answer came, except that the Miss Gubbingses were engaged, and would send one in the morning.

As the evening advanced Lady Lillyford's spirits seemed to revive a little from the shock they had sustained, and she began to talk of the engagement she had made that morning; for, as she perhaps wisely observed, " it will do us all good to think of something else. Mrs. Winchfield is going to have such a delightful party to-morrow night. Tableaux and plays, and some of the best *partis* are going to act in them. She even hopes to have the young Marquis of Ulswater. She has got that handsome Mr. Stuart I remember you danced with at the first ball, and Mr. Ashton; and, let me see, there was one who is very rich indeed, and so clever—dear me, I forget his name, and yet I used to know him formerly. He is an excellent actor, she tells me; and she wants you, Beatrice, to act in one of the pieces. It's a tableau, I think; you would only have to sit still and say nothing, so it will not be difficult."

Sir Charles, who did not at all like her contemplated expedition to see Roland, rather caught at the idea of this party, and said,

"Well, I daresay Beatrice will do it very well; and—and as to the expedition, I hope you will think better of it, for though I'd much rather leave London, yet at all events you can remain here, and I can go off at once and see if I can do any good."

"Oh! poor Roland—but it will be cruel of me not to go and see him."

"Time enough," he said; "I fear he won't be able to get out yet awhile. Besides, after all, it may be of use to him, and serve as a warning for the future. I shouldn't wonder if it did."

Beatrice hoped it might; still, to her inexperienced mind there was something so very dreadful in the idea of a prison, that she could scarcely sleep that night, and awoke in a sad state of depression the next morning.

CHAPTER VI.

Lady Lillyford thinks better of it, and instead of visiting her Son in Prison, goes to the Party at Mrs. Winchfield's.

LADY LILLYFORD did think better of it, and agreed to remain—at all events, to go to Mrs. Winchfield's party that night. Sir Charles said he would go also, for he wished to see the effect produced by his daughter's extreme beauty. He began to think it would be a very good thing if she could marry some one of the rich young men he heard of going about. With all these difficulties around him, he would like to see her safely established in a comfortable and, if possible, a luxurious home. So they dined rather earlier, in order to have time to dress after dinner, that " their dresses might be fresher," Lady Lillyford said.

It is often asserted that men are less worldly than women—that there are fewer match-making fathers than mothers, and I believe it is true. Nevertheless, I have generally observed that when once a man sets earnestly to work, he proves a much more persevering and relentless match-maker than almost any woman.

This certainly was the case with Sir Charles Lillyford. He felt he ought not to have taken that house in London—he knew it was a great piece of folly, but having done so, he determined to make the most of it, and did not see why Beatrice should not take advantage of the gay season to secure a good husband with a good fortune, especially as she would have a bad chance at Oakhampton, in consequence of his wife having provokingly set her face against all their country neighbours. Roused from his normal, easy-going indifference by his son's imprudence, he set himself resolutely to look about and see what Beatrice could pick up. He half forgot and wholly disregarded the attentions shown by Arthur Brookfield at Rome the year before, and therefore never imagined Beatrice could remember them better. The Fates seemed to forward his suddenly-formed schemes, for that very evening, at Mrs. Winchfield's, his attention was arrested by seeing a tall and handsome, though, he was obliged to confess to himself, rather a *roué*-looking man talking to his daughter. That he admired Beatrice there was no doubt; and from the embarrassment in her manner, and the colour in her cheeks, he fancied that she received his attentions with pleasure. On coming closer up to them, he recognised an old acquaintance, Sir Bevan Desborough. For a moment a suspicion that he was not worthy of her troubled him; but he remembered having heard that he was very well off now, and, after all, was old enough to have sown his wild oats, so that he might very likely prove as good a husband as other people. Then he joined in the conversation, and was glad to find they were to act together in one of the tableaux.

"We'll make up a dinner-party for him," he said to himself; "he's over head and ears in love with her already, that's quite plain—I shouldn't wonder if he proposes before the evening is out."

He was quite right. Sir Bevan Desborough was as much in love as it was possible for a thoroughly selfish and grovelling nature to be. And "he didn't see why he shouldn't marry the girl." It need not be any hindrance to certain habits which he might find it difficult to leave off, and she would be useful to give respectability to his fine country place and town house. Besides, he had a stronger motive still—he had discovered her secret, and was determined to cut out that hated rival, who knew more of his secrets than he liked.

But he possessed far too much knowledge—superficial knowledge, at least—of womankind, to propose that evening. He would allow her parents to advocate his cause first, and, by an appearance of backwardness, excite their anxiety and induce them to wish still more for the match. So he was respectfully admiring in his manner towards her, only endeavouring to make her feel less apprehensive and more at her ease with him than during their drive home from the City.

The tableau in which they appeared was rapturously applauded and encored.

Clemmy Gubbings, who had sent no answer to Beatrice's note, was not there—but Meely was, and said her sister was very unwell. Meely appeared in less good humour than usual, and Beatrice surprised a very malignant expression on her face while Sir Bevan Desborough was talking to her.

"You are not so fond of Miss Gubbings as you are of her sister," said he, when he saw Meely's black looks directed against

Beatrice. "I agree with you, she is not half so pleasant, and moreover is jealous of every-one who is better and prettier than herself. By-the-by, did you ever see their mother?" he said, while his eyes rested with a scruti-nizing expression on her face; "I believe you have—and I begin to suspect what the journey into the City was about. Oh, forgive me—I shall keep your secret, never fear—but I should like to know what mischief Miss Clemmy was at—and tried to drag you into also. She was secret enough about it."

Before they left the party Sir Charles had arranged that Sir Bevan was to dine with them the next day. "Only two or three old friends," he said. "No party."

Beatrice heard the invitation given and accepted, and her heart sank with a dreadful fear. She could scarcely define it—but it was as if a spell—a net were weaving round her, from the meshes of which she would be unable to escape.

This apprehension was if possible increased

during their drive home, for both parents were so warm in their praises of Sir Bevan.

"He has such a beautiful place in —— shire," said Sir Charles.

"I am sure he would gladly pay Roland's debts and get him out of prison," said Lady Lillyford, as she kissed Beatrice with unwonted affection, *à propos* to nothing, in a manner that filled the poor girl with alarm.

"I never saw such a case of love at first sight!" continued the delighted mother— "never—and so respectful; really if he thought you were a queen, he could not have shown more deference. He quite worships the ground you tread on."

Beatrice burst into tears, and the horrible idea of what might be expected from her filled her with grief and terror. She remembered, too, that Arthur Brookfield was not very rich—he certainly would not be able to get her brother out of prison. She found out he had never called all that day, and therefore, as he knew she was in London, he could not care to see her again. Perhaps he was actually married; but oh! nothing would induce her ever to accept that dreadful man. It was "quite impossible— quite!"

CHAPTER VII.

The Old Housekeeper's Shrewd Remarks.

WE left Mrs. Somerton returning from Oakhampton Hall, not having found the housekeeper at home, and having left the note for her containing Sir Charles's written permission to have the cabinet broken open. She appointed to come the next day, and begged the locksmith might meet her there; which message the housekeeper's niece, who opened the door, promised faithfully to deliver.

On their way home, she intended to call at the Vicarage, in the vague hope that the Mordaunts would have something to tell. She knew that anything was better than uncertainty to a mind like Elfrida's. The mental fatigue of hope and fear, the process of imagining and preparing oneself for, or reasoning away, all kinds of painful contingencies, and endeavouring to vanquish unreasonable fears, must go far to undermine the vital power of one whose feelings are at all times too powerful for the bodily strength. And it would have been to Elfrida an almost unendurable trial had she not habitually taught herself to say, with its awfully real meaning, "Thy will be done." She had been early taught (not to say, but) to pray with true reverence of belief, the full, sufficient, and deep meaning of the Lord's Prayer.

On arriving at the Vicarage, Peggy met them at the door, but she had no particular news to tell.

"Another weary day of suffering and uncertainty must be lived through; and," added Peggy, "there is no hope of hearing anything from the Miss Fairleighs, for they have gone rather unexpectedly to London. The chance of our knowing whether they received any letter from their brother is thus cut off."

"And there may be a letter at Ferncote now waiting for them, or forwarded by to-day's post," said Mrs. Somerton to the Vicar.

"Very likely—I will go and walk there to inquire," said Mr. Mordaunt, " the butler will know whether any one with a foreign post-mark has arrived; that I will,—or stay," he added, looking compassionately on Elfrida's pale cheeks, " as the day is so fine, I will give Peggy a drive, and you will both come with us—we will all go. The sight of that beautiful park, the consoling power that there is in nature's loveliest scenes, will do us good; the cawing of the rooks, the song of the early spring birds, the bursting hedge-rows, will soothe and cheer us. You will stop to luncheon, and then I will get the nice little open carriage from the village inn—I call it my carriage, for we use it whenever we drive out, and I find it much less trouble than keeping one."

So they started, and the Mordaunts and Mrs. Somerton had the pleasure of seeing that Elfrida, for whom this little excursion was devised, did her best to enjoy the sweet bracing air, and fully appreciated the lovely scenery through which they passed.

"What *are* we to say to the butler?" inquired Mr. Mordaunt, as they drove up the long avenue which led to Ferncote. "What excuse shall we give for calling at all, when we know the ladies have gone to London?"

"Say that we are anxious to hear news of some friends with whom Mr. Fairleigh is now staying, relations of Mrs. Somerton, and that there was a report that the bride was dead or lost," said Peggy. "Mr. Snodgrass is very civil, as I think really good gentlemen's servants usually are; and we will ask for their address in London, too. I will write and tell them to let us know all the news they can from Hohenstein."

Mrs. Somerton smiled at the straightforward readiness of Peggy's suggestion, for she felt convinced that the rest of the party, including herself, were so painfully absorbed in their anxieties about Edward Luscombe's fate and motives, that they almost forgot the natural excuses they possessed for desiring news of their relatives at Hohenstein.

They found the butler had gone with the ladies to London; they then asked to see the housekeeper, whereupon a portly woman, in an irreproachably white cap, made her appearance; and to their inquiries, replied that a letter with a foreign post-mark had arrived by the second post the evening before, and that she had re-directed and posted it at once. "Because," she added, "I knew well enough my young ladies was wishing to hear from master, and was always in hopes he'd say he was a-coming home, they was. And so we all be sure enough, and that he has found some nice young lady for his missus, we be."

The housekeeper cast a longing glance at

Elfrida as she said this, which plainly said that, as far as her opinion went, he would not have far to go to find a suitable wife.

"Unless she have got a sweetheart, which goes contrary," added the venerable dame to herself, as she noticed Miss Somerton's saddened countenance.

For people brought up like this old housekeeper are often more quick in their readings of countenance than the so-called better-educated and higher ranks—at least, I have often observed this to be the case. And this individual matron was a great gossip, fond of speculating upon and talking about the concerns and characters of her superiors.

"When do you expect the ladies back?" asked Mrs. Somerton.

"There's no knowing. They said they'd hurry back, says they, but lawk, I knows well what it is when they gets among friends, and my ladies have a power o' friends. Long afore they were rich (God bless 'em!)

and we lived at Brandon afore master comed
of age, and so they'd only a small allowance
for his edication like, and I was a'most maid
of all work; for though we'd two others they
didn't do half a day's work between them,
and I couldn't see my missus want for nothing; so, after their father died, I did the
work of all three, I did. And the neighbours
looked down upon them like at first, but
lawk, they soon learnt to know who was
who, and they was always a-coming and sending to drive them out, and have them in all
the great houses far and near. They were
as pop'lar as the Queen herself could have
been. But then when we come here, and
got all decent like and grand about them,
the folk at that there Hall opposite didn't
even so much as leave a card at their door.
'Tis hall hignorance, says I to Mr. Snodgrass;
and he says, says he, they've never learnt
'haviour, with living in foreign parts, and
don't know nothing about nobody. How-
somedever that may be, says I, I know them

Lillyfords won't never prosper all along of being so uncivil to my young ladies. But if my ladies was to stay in Lunnon, where I hear them Lillyfords are gone, they'd see then which has the best of it. They'll have a Countess and a Marchioness and a Duchess, for all I know a-leaving their cards at my ladies's door, and sending them opera and play tickets, as they did afore when they was poor; and now I'm sure that Mr. What's-his-name, that foreigneering-looking fellow, which is their butler down at Oakhampton Hall, won't have to open the door to half as many great people, he won't. For I saw Lady Lillyford's face once, and said I, that's not such a one as them real quality likes. But I be keeping of you out here, when I know Miss Fairleigh would be angry if you don't come in and have some luncheon, and take a turn in the garden and pick some flowers."

But they declined the old dame's hospitality, and having written down Miss Fairleigh's address in London, drove home.

Mr. Mordaunt advised Mrs. Somerton to write herself to Miss Fairleigh, as it was more natural that she should feel anxious about her relations at Hohenstein. This she accordingly did on their return home.

CHAPTER VIII.

Mrs. Somerton finds Oakhampton exactly like
her dream.

THE next morning being quite fine, Mrs.
Somerton and her daughter started
immediately after breakfast for Oakhampton.

"Strange! This is just as I dreamed it
was," said the former as they followed the
housekeeper up the carved oak staircase, and
saw the grotesque figures on the corners of
the landing-places, just as she had described
them to Elfrida. She pointed out the door
of the burnt room, and could have found the
late Lady Lillyford's bed-room without the
aid of the housekeeper.

There, standing in the very same corner,
and with the same slanting sunbeams tinging

the edges of its grotesque and gilded figures
—just as Mrs. Somerton had seen it in her
dream—they found the Indian cabinet. The
door had been already opened. At once
Mrs. Somerton proceeded to draw out a
small drawer on the left side—there were
twelve in each row, besides long ones. As
she expected, nothing was in it, but after
taking it quite out, as quickly as her shaking
hand would allow—for Mrs. Somerton was
extremely agitated—she pressed her trembling finger on a small knob, that was so
cleverly concealed at the farther corner, so
completely masked, that it would have been
impossible for anyone without a clue to have
found it out. She then carefully removed a
loose board, touched another spring at the
back of a drawer on the right side; a number of the other drawers then came out, and
disclosed a large space behind and below,
and, oh! the joy of that moment, it was
full of papers!

There was the packet directed to herself,

in the well known and much loved handwriting of her cousin ; there were the other manuscript papers, just as she had seen them in her strange dream. She took them out of their resting-place with shaking hands, and, too full of emotion to speak a word, she sat down on a sofa close by, and opened the packet more especially directed to herself. Giving a portion of it to her daughter, they were both soon so absorbed in perusing this bequest from the grave, so anxious to ascertain all the particulars of Lady Lillyford's sad history, that they might perhaps have remained there all the day, had not the housekeeper knocked at the door to know whether they would take any luncheon. Mrs. Somerton looked at her watch, and, startled to find that it was two o'clock, replied that she must return home at once. Then, thanking the old woman for her proffered hospitality, and gathering up the precious papers, they hastened home.

Mrs. Somerton was glad to see that their

perusal of Lady Lillyford's journal had served to beguile Elfrida during all those hours from the painful subject that weighed so heavily on them both; and as they had not read more than half, she hoped that the remainder would distract her attention during the rest of the day, and then perhaps to-morrow's post might bring from Miss Fairleigh some positive explanation of the rumours concerning Edward Luscombe and Dorina.

CHAPTER IX.

The Miss Fairleighs receive a Letter from their Brother.

THE old housekeeper at Ferncote was right in her surmises that the Miss Fairleighs would meet with many friends in London. Although their arrival had not been expected, yet as soon as it was known to some of their relations, invitations of all kinds had come pouring in. It was during this time that Miss Fairleigh was persuaded to take her young sister to the ball, where Rosa's likeness to Arthur Brookfield had startled Beatrice.

"In spite of my dislike to balls," said Miss Fairleigh, "I must confess I am glad that we went to Mrs. Dashville's, as it gave us the opportunity of seeing Miss Lillyford."

"Only the worst of it is," said Rosa, "that we shall never be happy now till they meet, and Arthur carries her safely away from that dreadful mother. Oh! if ever I disliked the looks of any one, 'tis that Lady Lillyford."

"Oh! Rosa!"

"I do. I will, and I can't help it. Such a dear, beautiful girl, and how longingly she looked at me. I know she was struck by the likeness to my brother. I am sure she cares very much for Arthur, and yet that cruel, worldly woman would not let her be introduced to us."

"Scarcely worldly, dear Rosa. Remember that Arthur has now such a large fortune, he surely——"

"Oh! but I daresay she wants rank or something of that kind for her daughter. And as far as that goes, she is worthy of any position, for she is so very beautiful."

"Yes, I am sure she is a dear good creature, and just made on purpose for Arthur," said Miss Fairleigh.

"And to think that mother of hers does not think him good enough! Of course she does not, when she knows how much he admired her daughter at Rome. If she had any wish to favour the match she would have called upon us."

"A thought has just struck me, dear Rosa. It is possible that after all Lady Lillyford may not have heard of our—of Arthur's change of name."

"Oh! that is quite impossible; and yet, now I come to think of it, they say Lady Lillyford is a very stupid as well as prejudiced woman; and certainly stupid people do contrive not to hear or see things, in a most miraculous manner. Oh! if I had thought that, I would have forced myself upon that lovely girl. I was very nearly speaking to her, and I really think if I had met her again, I could not have resisted it. It is really a pity we did not stay in town, now that you fancy this; for I am so afraid they may marry her to some one else—and this would be very sad, for she is the first person that has ever made any impression on Arthur."

This conversation passed at the country house (called Langton Hall) belonging to friends of the Miss Fairleighs, Mr. and Mrs. Stanway, with whom they were staying on their way home.

Mrs. Stanway was Mr. Sterndale's aunt (he who has been already introduced to the reader at Hohenstein as Arthur Fairleigh's companion in travel), and therefore she knew Arthur Fairleigh well—in fact, he was a great favourite of hers, and she was much interested in all that concerned him.

At breakfast, on the morning after this conversation took place, Miss Fairleigh received a letter from her brother, with the London postmark on it.

"Oh! how delightful!" exclaimed Rosa.

"Then Arthur must have returned home at last!"

The two sisters eagerly devoured the contents of the letter, and while they read it together their countenances denoted so much perplexity and annoyance that Mrs. Stanway, who sat opposite to them at the breakfast-table, noticed it. She knew they had been eagerly expecting their brother to arrive in England, had heard Rosa's exclamation, and was going to express her hopes that he would come and visit them before the sisters left their house. When they appeared to have read the important document, Mrs. Stanway said, as if she had not noticed the unpleasant impression produced by the letter,

"Will not your brother come and see us here before you all return home? You know how pleased we should be to see him, and hear from his own lips the wonderful adventures he and John Sterndale have had, and all they saw in those extraordinary caves. I declare that some of John's letters were like a fairy tale, and reminded me of the ' Arabian Nights.' "

Mrs. Stanway purposely went on talking for a few moments to allow the sisters time to recover from the embarrassment and perplexity they evinced.

"Oh! dear Mrs. Stanway," exclaimed Rosa, as she burst into tears, " I can't help it, for I am so disappointed. Now, don't look displeased with me, dear Louisa, pray; you know, I never can conceal anything from those whom I consider friends, so do let me cry, and you can tell, or not, what is the cause of—my disappointment."

The elder sister looked grave, and remained silent for a moment; then turning to Mrs. Stanway, said,

" Well, as I know you and Mrs. Stanway are such real friends, I can't see the harm; therefore poor Rosa, and indeed myself, need not be deprived of your kind sympathy. It is this—that we fear poor Arthur has now no chance of happiness in the quarter where we had hoped he would find it."

She then explained to Mrs. Stanway how he had long been attached to a very beautiful girl, but had been withheld from proposing to her before his tour in the East, because he did not feel sure that he had won her heart, and in fact he fancied that she was as yet too young. But he found that since his long tour abroad, and the varied scenes through which he passed, time had, if possible, strengthened his attachment, and he had become daily more anxious to win her heart. She also explained to Mrs. Stanway how much he had desired that herself and Rosa should become acquainted with the young lady, whose father had inherited a place near Ferncote, and that they should find out whether she retained any recollection of him; further, how her strange mother had frustrated this plan by not calling on them; that still he went on hoping, and was resolved to try and see the young lady as soon as he arrived in England; that when he heard she had gone to London, he hastened there on purpose.

"Oh! but, dear Julia, remember it may be all a mistake—he may find out that it was not her fault," interposed Rosa. "He ought not to have judged and condemned her so hastily. He was wrong. He ought to have followed the carriage and spoken to her; for I am sure those beautiful eyes of hers could never deceive. I am certain she is everything that is good and charming, and I have never found myself wrong about countenances."

"You have seen her, then?" inquired Mrs. Stanway.

"Yes; and I am certain she loves my brother, because she was evidently struck with the likeness between myself and him, and never took her eyes off me all the evening."

"And how—when did you meet her?"

"It was at Mrs. Dashville's ball," said the

elder sister, with a blush, for she knew that Mrs. Stanway was aware of her prejudices, and she was therefore all the more resolved to expose her own delinquency. " At the only ball I ever was at," she went on to say; " and I must confess I was extremely pleased with her. I should indeed regret most deeply if——"

" But you have not told me the impediment ?—what can it be ? Surely your brother's position is such as to satisfy her parents—she cannot have refused him ?"

" No; but it seems he met her driving out without her mother, with a gentleman who he has reason to know is a man of the very worst character ; and seeing her under these peculiarly strange circumstances, the only explanation he thinks possible must be, that she is engaged to be married to that horrid man !"

" Surely that is most unlikely," said Mrs. Stanway ; " but really, men who are deeply in love are such fools, there is no knowing what nonsense they may not take into their heads. "Yes," she added, nodding to her husband across the breakfast-table, "you know I am right—you know you were just as bad. You fancied all manner of things before we were engaged, but, alas!" she added, with mock concern, "he never takes it into his head to be jealous now. I might go and drive in Hansoms with the greatest swells, as they call them, in London, and he would not care a bit. I daresay this catastrophe of your brother's is some mistake or other."

"Well, it is possible," said Miss Fairleigh, trying to smile; "but whatever it is, it has had the effect of making him leave London without making any effort to see her, and the consequence, of course, will be that she will—that she must think that he does not care for her; and her mother is such a strange, and, I suppose, worldly woman, that she, perhaps, will wish her to marry this good-for-nothing man; and as my brother has been so long coming forward, the poor girl herself may think that he has forgotten her."

"Oh! I am sure that would never occur to her," said Rosa. "Stay, let us look at the date of his letter—17th!—why, it was only posted the 19th, so he must have left town the day before yesterday. Ah! I suppose at the tiresome hotel they never posted it till the day after—a trick so often played there."

"Then he must have gone to Ferncote yesterday. Why, Rosa, we ought to return at once, though he tells us not; but he will feel so lonely at that new place all by himself."

"Ah! yes," said Rosa, "of course we must go, as he says he cannot come here."

"Why not?—let us write and try to persuade him," said Mrs. Stanway. "Besides," she added, when she saw that Miss Fairleigh looked determined to go, "you can't start till to-morrow, for there is no train that will arrive, except at night. Besides, the second post may perhaps bring a letter from your brother to say he is coming; it arrives at two, and we will send in on purpose to Langton Bridge. It would be too provoking," she continued, " if your visit is cut so short; and if your brother will not come here, I'm sure he will find plenty to do to interest him in that beautiful Ferncote. I remember it when I was staying at Oakhampton many years ago. By-the-by, I think I have divined who the beautiful young lady is. Ah! I see I have, for I have heard of her beauty from my old friend, Mrs. Manderton. She keeps me *au fait* of all the news, and describes the new beauties in her pleasant letters; and she described that young lady, and regretted that her mother was such a goose, and her brother such a hopeless *roué* and gambler, that she is afraid he will soon ruin the family."

CHAPTER X.

Strange News contained in a Gossiping Letter.

THE second post brought no letters from Arthur, but there was one for Mrs. Stanway from this very Mrs. Manderton.

" Now we shall have all the latest news," said Mrs. Stanway, as she sat down by the fire to read it comfortably in her arm-chair, and began to read it aloud. " 'We were persuaded for the first time to go to a party at Mrs. Winchfield's, as I had heard that her character had been unjustly aspersed ; but I am sorry we did, for there was a very bad set, and I was sorry to see that pretty girl, Miss Lillyford, there—' Oh !" exclaimed Mrs. Stanway, stopping short, and then reading on for a few minutes in silence.

"What is it?" inquired Rosa; "I am sure she says something about Miss Lillyford—now do,tell us the facts."

Having read to the end of her letter, Mrs. Stanway said:

" Well, as you wish it, I will read exactly what she says.   'I was sorry to see that pretty Miss Lillyford acting in a *tableau* with that most worthless man, Sir Bevan Desborough.' "

" Ah ! Louisa, the very name," exclaimed Rosa.

" Shall I go on?" said Mrs. Stanway.

" Oh! yes, pray do."

" 'And that he seemed evidently on terms of intimacy with her. Once I saw them whispering together, as if they had some secret; and, in fact, this morning old Sir James Irwin called and told me that he had proposed that very evening, and that Miss Lillyford was going to be married to him. You know Sir James, though he is a Paul Pry, generally contrives to find out the truth. So I'm very much afraid that the beauty of the season is really going to be thrown away. Lady Horatia told him that her brother was thrown into prison for debt; that his father is ruined; so that Sir James Irwin seems to think it probable that the poor girl will sacrifice herself, as he has offered to pay all the debts if she will consent to marry him, but they are not to be paid till her wedding-day."

"Oh! poor girl—how dreadful!" said Rosa.

The letter went on to say that "the Gubbings girls are in some way mixed up in it; that Clemmy Gubbings has long been attached to Roland Lillyford, and if his debts are paid she will marry him. It is said that she has helped to make up this match of Sir Bevan's with the beauty, and her sister has quarrelled with her in consequence, as she wanted to marry Sir Bevan herself; and that Lady Horatia Nolan came to London, and found them all at sixes and sevens, and is furious with them all, as she herself wanted to marry the young spendthrift, who is very handsome; and she vows she will be avenged on those Gubbings girls, and turn them quite out of society. Clemmy declares she doesn't care, but the eldest, " Meely," is heartbroken, and declares she will go and live abroad, and spite all her friends. So you see there is quite a tragedy going on in the world; but everybody pities that beautiful girl, and yet I must say that at Mrs. Winchfield's party she did not seem so unwilling to favour him as I fancied she ought, if she knew his character. But she probably does not, and will now, of course, be kept in the dark. by her friends, and not discover her mistake till it is too late."

" Oh! Louisa, what can we do?" exclaimed Rosa, when Mrs. Stanway had finished reading the letter.

" Surely she ought to be undeceived. Could not Mrs. Somerton write to her? She knows what kind of man Sir Bevan Desborough is, for I know she was at Naples the same season he was there. Yes—we will get her to write."

"Easily said," answered Louisa, "but I think it probable her letter might never reach the person for whom it was intended. You know they would not let her meet them at Oakhampton."

"Not meet the Somertons !" exclaimed Mrs. Stanway—"why, Mrs. Somerton is sought for by all the best people everywhere. What an extraordinary woman that Lady Lillyford must be !"

"Yes; therefore, you see, it would never do for Mrs. Somerton to meddle in this sad case."

"No," said Mrs. Stanway, "I don't see that anything can be done. If the young lady is so weak as to be persuaded——"

"It would not be weakness, I am certain," said Rosa, indignantly. "Quite the reverse. I'm sure she would only sacrifice herself from the highest feelings of duty, to save her family from ruin."

"That may be," said Mrs. Stanway; "still I maintain a woman has no right to marry a man she cannot love—it is a positive crime; and I can't help thinking that with all those debts and imprisonments, and the brother's worthlessness, your brother will have had rather an escape. You know I have always had a wife in my eye for him, and still more have I wished it since he got this place near them."

"Who is that?"

"Can't you guess? That pretty clever daughter of a celebrated Mother, who I know will make the most perfect of wives, but I believe you did not know her till you went to Ferncote. Your brother met them at Rome, and there too I saw a great deal of both; I was always saying she is quite cut out for your brother."

"She is very charming; but there is a sadness about her,—I fancy she loved somebody, and that it went wrong: I have an idea that Arthur knows the person," added Rosa.

"Oh, I hope she has had no disappointment," said Mrs. Stanway, " for she has such deep feelings and such fragile health, I am afraid she is one of those who could scarcely survive—one who even might die of a broken heart."

"Only that I believe she has been so well and religiously trained," said Miss Fairleigh ; "although Mrs. Somerton does not agree with all my views of religion, I can see that she is a most true Christian."

"Now I hope you will bring them here soon," said Mrs. Stanway. "I mean that as I know they are poor they could not perhaps come alone. You must tell Mrs. Somerton that she shall have a study all to herself to write her books in, and shall not have to see anyone unless she feels quite well and in the humour for it. How I envy you having them so near you."

CHAPTER XI.

Arthur Fairleigh is determined to be miserable and to believe the worst.

THE two sisters left Langton Bridge the next morning by an early train, and arrived quite late at Ferncote, for they had a long distance to travel. They found their brother waiting for them at the station with the carriage, for he felt sure they would come, he said.

He looked worn and anxious, yet endeavoured to give them a cheerful welcome, and expressed the great admiration and delight he felt at the beautiful place which had so unexpectedly become their home. He expatiated upon its various merits, and upon the advantages of having such good, agreeable neighbours,—among others, Mr. Mordaunt and the Somertons. These he had already seen and was charmed with them. " They made me feel that I really was coming to my home," he said.

During the drive nothing was mentioned about the subject which was uppermost in all their minds; but when they had all three entered the comfortable and well-lighted library (for it had been dark long before they reached the Park), he pointed to a newspaper with a trembling hand, and said,

" You will see there that my fears—my worst fears are confirmed."

Rosa seized it hurriedly, and read the following paragraph :—

"A marriage is arranged, and will shortly take place, between Sir Bevan Desborough and the beautiful and accomplished daughter of Sir Charles Lillyford, the acknowledged belle of the season."

" Oh ! Arthur, don't allow it," exclaimed

Rosa; " I am sure she loves you ;" and then she related having met her at Mrs. Dashville's ball, and how Beatrice had watched her all the evening; and she also told him what Sir James Irvine had said to Mrs. Manderton about the father and brother, and their debts. But Arthur shook his head, and assumed that stern air which had often frightened her in her wayward childhood; and both sisters perceived that the subject must not be mentioned again.

"I was wrong to show you this," said he, when he perceived their grave and sorrowful faces. "It was very selfish of me to intrude my grief at this joyful moment of our meeting in this beautiful home, particularly as our poor neighbours the Somertons have, I fear, still greater cause for sorrow. I promised Mr. Mordaunt that you would go and see them to-morrow morning."

" What about their cousin—that unfortunate bride? Mrs. Somerton wrote to me in London to inquire if I had heard from you.   Well, and what did you hear before you left Hohenstein?"

"The Gräfin had not been found, nor could any intelligence be got anywhere as to her fate.   But there was a strange story about a letter or paper which had been posted up in the mountains the south side of Gratz, which one of the students to whom it was shown, maintains to be Edward Luscomb's writing.   When I left Sterndale, who is always called a travelling justice of the peace—for he will sift matters to the bottom—he was determined to go there and ascertain the origin and meaning of the report. There is an idea that if they were lost in the cave and did not die, they must have fallen into the hands of some band of smugglers or robbers who infest some of its secret outlets and carry on their illicit trade.   If so, they will not allow them to escape, for fear the secret of their haunts should become known."

"Then you don't think it was a preconcerted plan and they meant to elope? That idea seemed to be what weighed most heavily with the Somertons."

" I cannot think it possible, but I know there was one person who wished it might be so, and who favoured the view. In fact, I strongly suspect that she caused the report of the two being seen together on horseback to be circulated ; and so does Sterndale."

" What, that cousin, I suppose, with whom we began to fear you were falling in love ?"

" She is a most wonderfully captivating girl, but I was sufficiently cool to watch her narrowly. Such a power of will, too ! It is fortunate for the world at large that she is not a queen, or a cabinet minister's wife, for she would turn the whole world topsy-turvy, and sacrifice her best friend, if he stood in her way."

" And I suppose she wants to marry the bereaved bridegroom—is that her plan ?"

" I suppose so ; but the idea is so revolting one cannot bear to believe it possible. Such a lovely bride, so devotedly attached to the Count, and yet so confidingly fond of her cousin. She would never believe anything against her."

"And was the Count as much devoted to her, or will he get over her loss, do you think?"

"I should say never," said Arthur, in a tone of sadness, that showed plainly the word found an echo in his own heart; but he added, turning away, "There is no knowing how Cunigunda may endeavour to work upon him, if that is her game."

CHAPTER XII.

Lady Lillyford is in the full enjoyment of choosing her Daughter's Trousseau.

"SATIN, or this rich brocade? I think satin, for it will show off that lovely Brussels point best. You know Sir Bevan sent to Brussels on purpose for it. The finest and most costly ever made."

"It is magnificent, indeed. Then, if you choose satin for Beatrice, I will fix on this rich brocade, and I will have it made quite plain and simple. Don't you advise that, Madame Rosalie?"

"*Mais oui.* I do think it best suit Mademoiselle's *tournure;* but she will have one ver' wide row of lace down de side, wid the bouquet of orange, and one single pearl in *chacune?*"

"A very good idea. Now, dear Lady Lillyford, as to the going-away dress, what do you think of this lovely mauve for darling Beatrice? Do look at it, darling! I am sure you must admire this lovely brocade. Ah! she has got such a sad headache. Well, never mind, dearest, we won't bother you; your mamma and I will settle it all."

This conversation was overheard by a gentleman who was choosing some artificial flowers at the other end of the room. He turned round suddenly, and scanned the two speakers, and the pale, sad-looking girl, whose opinion on the weighty matter was appealed to in vain. He gazed on them with a pair of dark, searching eyes, as if he meant to read them through and through.

Lady Lillyford and Clemmy were evidently too much occupied with their important selections to notice his scrutiny. But Beatrice had been looking at a delicate girl, who was holding up the flowers for him to choose from, and thus became aware that his attention was arrested by herself; or, rather, she felt, perhaps, half pleased at the look of deep compassion with which he regarded her.

It was only a moment, for as soon as her eyes met his, he turned to the pale girl and her blush roses, selecting one of the wreaths. He then wrote down something on a slip of paper, which he gave to the girl, and, on reading it, she too gazed at Beatrice, and with something of the same compassionate expression. The gentleman then left the room, and Beatrice, who had felt interested by the face of that girl, even when she first came into the room, now went over and looked at the flowers. The girl smiled, as if she were pleased at seeing her flowers noticed, but did not speak; and there was something in her manner which made Beatrice fancy she was deaf and dumb, probably because she rather resembled a little girl she used to meet at Naples, in the Villa Reale, when she was a child, who was deaf and dumb, and who had then interested her very much.

The girl pointed out some very lovely azalias, and held them up to Beatrice, who expressed her admiration both by words and looks. She then seized some orange flowers which lay near, and made a quick gesture of dislike, pushing them away, and frowning at them, while her lips seemed to try to say the word "No, no." Then, seeing another lady approach, she resumed her usual weary look, and proceeded listlessly to settle the disarranged flowers.

"Oh! are you selecting the wreath, darling?" inquired Lady Lillyford, with a pleased look. "Here, show us the orange-flower wreaths," she said, in a commanding tone, to the flower-girl.

"She does not hear—I remember now," said Clemmy, "she is deaf and dumb; but she is very quick, and guesses often by the motion of the lips what one wants. Show us some bridal wreaths," she said, speaking very distinctly with her lips.

Beatrice thought she saw an expression of anger or contempt on the girl's face, while she pulled out some drawers and displayed some of the largest wreaths before Clemmy.

"I think that this with the dew-drops would suit me best; but we shall want two alike—have you not another?"

The girl shook her head with something of the same angry look.

" But you can get another made like this?"

Again the girl shook her head more resolutely than before. .

"But I'm sure you can," said Clemmy. "Oh! she's stupid to-day, I can't make her understand—I must speak to one of the other girls; but we have no more time to-day. Now, come, or we shall be late," said she, turning to Lady Lillyford. " Come, Beatrice, don't be loitering among those flowers with that stupid girl."

"She looks so very intelligent," said Beatrice, " I feel quite interested by her.   She must be an Italian, I should think, by her large dark eyes and olive complexion."

" I think she is—the Neapolitans are wonderful flower-makers, I believe."

"Then I daresay it is—it may be the very same I remember at Naples.   How I should like to know."

CHAPTER XIII.

Beatrice is again reminded of Naples.

THE next morning, when Beatrice was walking in the Square with Clemmy (she was never permitted to go there alone now), she saw the same tall gentleman who looked at her with so much compassion in Madame Rosalie's show-room. He was sitting under the trees reading, but as she passed, he again looked at her with a compassionate but deeply respectful air.

" Who can that be?" said Clemmy. " One so seldom sees strangers here—such a distinguished-looking man too. Perhaps it is Lord Fitzwilfred, who has taken the corner house. His face seems familiar to me."

In the course of their walk round the

Square they passed again near the bench where he sat.

" But, my gracious !" said Clemmy, " how stern and angry he looked at me. Ah ! you were looking the other way, and did not see him. Where can I have seen that face, I wonder ? I don't think now he is a London man."

" He somehow reminds me of Naples," said Beatrice. " It must have been many years ago that I saw him there."

" Yes," said Clemmy, " I dare say—who can he be ?" And then she was silent; looking anxious and unhappy, as she often did when she was not talking, or endeavouring to keep up the drooping spirits of Beatrice.

Clemmy was living with them now ; for she had quarrelled with her sister, or rather, as Clemmy described it, " Meely turned me out of the house—she was so angry at my being constant to poor dear Roland. I shall be a martyr for his sake," she often said.

The third time they passed the stranger Beatrice purposely did not look in the direction; but as her head was not turned away, she half saw and half felt that he was gazing fixedly on her, with the same kind of compassion which had at first arrested her attention at Madame Rosalie's the day before.

" What can it be ?" she wondered; " and why did the poor, pale, interesting flower-girl look just the same at me after he gave her a slip of paper to read, on which he wrote something ?"

In her depth of despair she felt grateful for any sympathy, and a kind of vague hope was excited in her by seeing that stranger's resolute look of compassion. His features were strongly marked, though not at all handsome; and he had an air of determination and rectitude, which probably tended to inspire her with hope; for she felt, more than reasoned or thought, that she was being treated with extreme injustice.

And in order better to explain the position

of Beatrice, we must now take the reader back about three weeks.

Unfortunately her grandmother had been absent from London during this time—in fact, ever since the fatal expedition to the City. She had been detained in Yorkshire by the dangerous illness of a niece, whom she had gone to visit.

Beatrice had written several times, and detailed all the difficulties which surrounded her,—how her father and Lady Lillyford had appealed to her generosity to save her brother from ruin; how her mother had reproached her for selfishness when she extracted from her the secret of her constancy to Arthur Brookfield.

Lady Lillyford had said,

"For shame! I wonder you haven't more proper pride than to fall in love that way with a man who never so much as proposed, and who never comes near you now, though you say you saw him one day, so he must be in England. For of course if he had the slightest affection for you he would not have lost a day in calling."

"But—but," said the perplexed Beatrice, "he may have heard that—that I was going to marry someone else."

"He could not have heard it then; besides, do you think he would be such a fool as not to come and see with his own eyes, and hear with his own ears, whether the report was true? Nonsense, don't be so ungrateful as to sacrifice us all. I'm ashamed of you for thinking of such a thing, and your want of proper pride. There, don't cry now, or you'll make your eyes quite red, and you ought to be so grateful that in all our misfortunes you have found a husband who not only loves you, and will give you beautiful horses and carriages and jewels, and I don't know what, and is so very generous as to save your brother besides. But it's my belief that you'd rather see us all go to prison than deny yourself the smallest gratification. Why can't you take example from

Clemmy, who has been turned out of her sister's house and incurred martyrdom—as she herself says—all for the sake of saving Roland, and because——"

"Because she loves him, mamma; and you want me to sacrifice all my—yes, best feelings and wishes, to marry a man I hate—yes, I do hate him; I never knew what it was to hate before."

Lady Lillyford stopped her ears, and went off in one of her hysterical fits. And Beatrice was obliged to ring for the maid, and Clemmy came and reproached her for killing her mother with her obstinacy.

CHAPTER XIV.

Will she be entangled in the net they are
weaving around her.

BEATRICE described some of the scenes she had undergone several times to Mrs. Dronington, and implored her to come and advise her what to do. But no answer had arrived, and she felt that some one, either Clemmy or her mother, was always watching her. She at last began to fear that by some strange contrivance they had prevented her letters going to the post. She began to feel gradually that she was treated like a prisoner. Clemmy slept in the room next to hers, and there was a door communicating between the two rooms, and she could never write a letter without fancying that Clemmy's piercing eyes were watching her.

At first she hoped to find an advocate in her father, because she had often felt that he understood her better than her mother did. But to her surprise and dismay she found that he was, if possible, still more anxious for the match.

"You should make hay while the sun shines," he said; "for there is no knowing how soon we may all go to jail."

"But surely there can be no danger—for your Oakhampton estate is——"

"Don't say another word," he exclaimed with an angry frown and look of despair which she never before had seen on his usually good-humoured face. "I—I—have a great mind to tell you all, only women never can keep a secret. But everybody is against us. It was all your mother's fault for making such a fuss with that confounded Lady Horatia. I always thought it foolish; it was her own doing, and now she has turned against us, and she has it in her power to do us all irreparable mischief."

"How? Why?"

"Because she was fool enough to fall in love with that boy, and now she vows vengeance against him for deserting her. But you saw yourself in that stationer's bill that she came after Clemmy, as far as that goes. She is a most dangerous woman, and she has taken something into her head; of course I mean she can prove nothing, but she threatens to tell people that she can; and if she persists we may be obliged to go to law and incur no end of expenses in establishing our rights. But remember, don't say anything of this to Clemmy, for I hope, I think she has not heard it; for between you and me, it it is all very well for her to talk of being a martyr for love. I don't think she would take all this trouble if she thought Roland had a chance of being cut out of his property and Baronetcy."

"But what could deprive him of that?"

"Never mind—only that I know you are more sensible than most girls or women, I

would not have said so much. I only wish
you to see we have a chance of being all
beggars."

Why should this be, she wondered; but her
own troubles, and the apprehension that she
should be obliged to accept Sir Bevan, were
so overwhelming, that she soon ceased to
think of her father's mysterious words.

As a last effort to escape, she thought of
appealing to the generosity of Sir Bevan
himself; she would tell him plainly that it
was quite impossible she could consent—that
she never, never could love him.

But this plan, too, failed; for he declared
he was quite satisfied—that he knew very
well that he was no longer of the age to expect a young girl's love, he only wished to
make her happy as best he could, and to save
her brother from ruin.

And so she had gradually been worked
upon to consider her fate inevitable, and to
behold the preparations going on in a kind of
dreamy state at times, as if scarcely aware

that her fate was thereby sealed. She went about listlessly to the shops, or wherever her mother or Clemmy took her; and a few days after her visit to Madame Rosalie's to choose the wedding-dress, she was glad to find that they intended going there again, for she wished to see the deaf and dumb girl.

CHAPTER XV.

They call at Madame Rosalie's about the Bridal Wreath.

"THEY have never sent us the other bridal wreath from Madame Rosalie's," said Clemmy; "we will go there to-day to see about it, and I want to give some directions about the blue *velours épinglé* dress; besides, my mauve body does not fit well at all."

As they drove through Brook Street, on their way to Madame Rosalie's, Clemmy exclaimed,

"Good gracious! there's that stern-looking man waiting at Lady Horatia's door, the man we saw in our Square."

Beatrice looked round with extreme curiosity, for she longed to see his compassionate glance fixed on her once more.

"I wonder what mischief he is concocting there?" added Clemmy. "I can fancy if those two resolute heads get together no good can come of it."

The hall door was opened just at that moment, so that Beatrice was only able to see that it was the same man; and the words her father had spoken about Lady Horatia's vindictiveness came into her mind.

"But surely," she thought, "that man who had looked at her so kindly could never mean to do them harm."

"I must find out who he is," said Clemmy; "did not you say you saw him at Madame Rosalie's one day, Beatrice?"

"Yes."

"Well, I wonder if he is known there. I will ask. Now, Trixey, do help to describe him—about six feet high, I should say, dark hair, and broad, straight, bushy eyebrows, fierce black eyes, square shoulders. That's it, is it not?"

"Yes, except the fierce eyes. I did not remark—I thought——"

"Well, what? Don't you think he has? I see you are as curious about him as I am, so you must help me to ask one of those 'young ladies' in the shop, as they call themselves," added Clemmy, with a contemptuous toss of her head.

It occurred to Beatrice that she had never seen any person more like a lady than that pale deaf and dumb girl. She felt quite pleased at the idea of seeing those expressive and compassionate eyes again.

She was not in the show-room, however, when they went in, and Clemmy for a time was too much absorbed in her trimmings and velvet and lace, to think of anything else, and so was Lady Lillyford, who, under the plea of making herself decent for her daughter's wedding, and the parties which were to be given afterwards, was getting a complete set of new and expensive dresses. It was her happiest moment when, having gathered round her in a heap the richest of laces, brocades, and trimmings, she could say to the shop people, with a condescending yet triumphant gesture, "Yes—I will have that." It was a pleasure she had never enjoyed to the like extent in all her life before.

In the meantime Beatrice was turning over the flowers, in hopes the deaf and dumb girl would appear; but she did not, until Clemmy, when she had finished with her dresses, came over, and said to one of the other girls in an angry tone,

"Why didn't you send the two wreaths we ordered?"

"I will inquire, ma'am; but I believe the delay was caused by Mamselle Fronica, the head flower-maker. I will go and inquire."

The girl went, and soon returned with the deaf and dumb girl, who seemed agitated, and looked more ill and pale than the pre-

ceding day.   The other one expressed that
she was very sorry to have disappointed the
ladies, and would be sure to finish and send
them to them the next day.

" Oh, very well," said Clemmy; and then
she began to ask who that gentleman was
who was buying flowers there the last day
they came?

The girl did not remember anything about
a gentleman, but she asked the deaf and
dumb girl if she remembered, and begged
her to write down the name if she could.
But Fronica shook her head, and tried to
express either that she did not understand
whom they meant or could not remember.

So Clemmy's curiosity was destined not to
be gratified, but as they were leaving the
room Beatrice turned round to take another
look at the pale face which interested her so
strangely, and saw a kind of triumphant
smile light up her expressive features. Fixing her eyes on Beatrice, she raised her
finger quickly to her lips and blew a kiss,

just as Beatrice had seen Neapolitan children
do. Then she pressed her finger to her
mouth in token of silence.

The gesture was so quick and slight that
it would scarcely have been observed, and
was, in fact, unnoticed save by Beatrice, and
one sharp-eyed girl who did not approve of
that Italian Mamselle, and did not see why
everybody should compassionate her, only
just because she couldn't hear or speak.

This girl (Miss Button) determined to find
out what secret there was between her and
Beatrice, particularly as she had overheard
Clemmy's inquiries about a tall, dark gentleman.

"I know well enough," muttered she,
"that he is a friend of Mademoiselle Fronica,
for I have observed him one or two times
before, when he had bought nothing, I believe, and only stuffed papers into her
hand."

And Miss Button strongly suspected that
the girl gave him some letter, but she was so

quick with her fingers there was no seeing.

As soon as the object of her dislike left the room, she said to one of the others,

"I don't wonder at those ladies wishing to know who that gentleman was, for I remember noticing him very much, and he's certainly some friend of Mamselle's, and doesn't come for any good, depend upon it, and never bought anything as far as I could see. If Mademoiselle Rosalie would ask, perhaps Fronica would be obliged to tell. Ah! you don't like to meddle, I see; you're all so kind to her, and think her quite a piece of perfection. Well, we shall see; if I ain't wrong she's a sly one, and no better than she should be."

CHAPTER XVI.

The Wreath is taken home; but Miss Button resolves not to lose sight of the Deaf and Dumb Girl.

THE wreath was finished that night, and Fronica begged Madame Rosalie's permission to take it herself to Lady Lillyford's house.

Miss Button was present when she made the request, and on hearing that it was readily granted, she said,

"Then I'll go there at the same time, with Miss Gubbings' mauve body, as she was so particular about it, and get her to try it on before I put the trimming."

Fronica perceived that she was to be accompanied by the girl whose good-will

she had failed to win, but though much disappointed she did not show it.

They were to go between six and seven
o'clock that evening. On arriving at Lady
Lillyford's door they saw a carriage waiting,
which Miss Button guessed was probably
that of the bridegroom-elect, Sir Bevan Desborough.

Fronica looked quickly at the arms, and
became so deadly pale, that had not her veil
been down and her face turned away, the
quick-eyed Button would have been struck,
and her curiosity still more excited.

The hall door was open, and Sir Bevan's
tall footman was laughing and talking with
those of Sir Charles, and the milliner's girls
with their band-boxes sat down to wait in
the hall whilst their arrival was reported to
the young lady's own maid. A few moments
afterwards the drawing-room bell rang, and
the footmen prepared their faces for their
master's coming down stairs.

Of course Miss Button looked round and

put on her most becoming expression—for bridegrooms must be temporary heroes of trousseau-makers.

" Very handsome and well preserved," was her mental comment, " but still I'd rather not be the lady who is to be his wife."

Miss Button's showy face and figure were not lost upon Sir Bevan.

" A handsome girl," thought he, but he scarcely noticed the small figure near, or marked how her delicate hands trembled as she tried to steady them by unfastening the knot in her flower-box; yet as he turned towards the door and left the hall, she raised her veil for a minute and gazed with a look of lingering curiosity after him. Then, in obedience to the message sent down from the young ladies, they proceeded up stairs.

They were shown into Miss Gubbings' room. and had full leisure to contemplate the litter of various kinds it contained. Miss Button's restless eyes glanced over several of the notes and letters that lay on the writing-table, for she always conceived it her duty to obtain all the information she could, as it was more useful to know things than to be ignorant of them. There was one letter she wished to finish, and had had dexterity enough to turn the page, when she heard the door open, and with great presence of mind she placed the carton she had brought over it on the table.

"Oh, I didn't know you wanted to try on anything more," said Miss Gubbings, in a rude tone, and rather cross at the martyrdom (as she called it—martyrdom was at present her pet word) of being fitted by the stupid milliner's girl; for those are often the most rude to those beneath them who have the least right to consider themselves better than others.

"I really begin to be sorry I did not go to Paris for my trousseau, they manage those things so much better there," she said.

"Well, Miss, I hardly think that, for Lady Horatia told Madame Rosalie herself, when

I were by, that she was obliged to drive three or four times to Mademoiselle Victorine's to have her things fitted, because they wouldn't send any of the young women out of her shop."

"And what did that girl come for?" said Clemmy; "surely if she's deaf and dumb she can't be of any use."

"It was at her own particular request," said Miss Button, with a significant emphasis, while her back was turned towards Fronica.

But she did not see that there was a looking-glass in which the deaf and dumb girl could read the strongly emphasized words, and also the look of anxiety which accompanied Clemmy's, "Oh, what can it be?—can't you find out?"

"I did think it was to see or say something to Miss Lillyford, 'cause I caught her making signs to her yesterday when you weren't looking."

"Oh! you did, did you?" and Clemmy looked sharply round to Fronica, and asked her, in a resolute and commanding way, what she wanted.

Fronica quickly pointed to the wreath she had brought, and did not seem to perceive that any other explanation was necessary.

"That can't be all; you wish to see Miss Lillyford, I suppose?"

Veronica nodded her head.

"And why?" asked Clemmy; "is it only to see how she likes your wreath? Well, though I much doubt if that is the case, I will call her."

"Come here, Trixey," she said, calling to the next room. "Here's this deaf and dumb girl wants to see you very particularly," and the lynx-eyed pair both watched Beatrice as she came in and looked with extreme pleasure on the pale face of the girl, saying in her simple tones,

"Oh! I'm so glad, for I like her so much" —and she added, turning to Fronica, "it was very good of you to bring it yourself."

Fronica shook her head, and waved her fore-finger to and fro before her face, in the true Neapolitan manner, expressive of strong negative.

Clemmy and Miss Button were both watching so intently, that although Beatrice felt sure the girl wished to express more without drawing upon herself the notice of the others, she was quite at a loss how to assist her.

But she took up a pencil and piece of paper from the table and said,

" I dare say you wish to tell us something about the wreath."

But again Fronica shook her head and motioned away the paper; then drawing her shawl close over her shoulders, she went towards the door as if she thought it time to go, while she directed an anxious and disappointed look towards Beatrice. The latter was however so convinced that she wanted to tell her something which the others were not to know, that she resolved to go into her own room, slip down by the back stairs, and then try to meet Fronica in the hall. But her design was most provokingly anticipated by both Clemmy and the other girl.

"Stay," said Miss Button, laying hold of Fronica's shoulder, and bringing her forcibly back. "Don't you see I haven't tried on the mauve body yet? Don't run away till I've done. You must help me to carry all these things home." And Clemmy said,

"Here, Trixey, do help me to take off this, and you must see how it sits. Now don't run away, there's a dear."

Beatrice therefore thought it better to remain and watch for some other opportunity before they left the house.

Clemmy and Miss Button chattered away very pleasantly while the operation was being performed, but Beatrice observed that they never for a moment lost sight of herself or Fronica.

"There, that will do beautifully, and it was

very lucky you came," said Clemmy in a far kinder tone.

It was wonderful to see how kind she had grown in her manner towards the dress-maker, since she had perceived that the latter was helping her to circumvent the obnoxious flower-girl.

" I am very glad you came;" and then she added in a low whisper, "and do find out what the girl wants with *her*, and come back and tell me."

Beatrice could not hear the words, but she saw that Fronica was able to comprehend them, for a faint smile played for a moment round her lips—but it did not reach the earnest and anxious expression of her eyes, which were fixed mournfully on Beatrice as she and her companion left the room.

" Oh, dear, how stupid—I left my purse in the drawing-room," exclaimed Beatrice, as if to furnish an excuse to Clemmy for going down stairs just after they were gone. "No—I think it was in the dining-room," added Beatrice, running down very fast, and passing the girls on the stairs. Clemmy was equally as quick and reached her at the door, but to the surprise of Beatrice she went into the dining-room and left her alone in the hall.

"Now," thought Beatrice, "if she has a note or anything to give me she may perhaps elude the vigilance of the other girl."

The plan was very nearly successful, for Miss Button did not come down stairs so fast as the other.

Fronica looked anxiously round, and then quickly drew a note from under her shawl. Beatrice knew it was for her, and was just going to take it, when unfortunately, owing to their agitation, it slipped from between their fingers, and being very small and light, was wafted a few feet away from them. Beatrice and Fronica both endeavoured to pick it up; but at that moment Miss Button's strong hand seized it, and she said, with great presence of mind,

" You are making a mistake—this note
was not intended for Miss Lillyford, Madame
Rosalie commissioned me to see it delivered
right, and I must do so."

Clemmy reappeared from the dining-room,
hearing the words, and begged Miss Button
to shew her what all the talking was about;
but she replied resolutely, " Oh, it's all a
mistake, ma'am; it was intended for Miss
Smith, to explain about her court dress not
being ready till to-morrow; and we must
take it to her at once. These foreigners
don't understand anything. It's lucky Madame Rosalie told me about it too."

Clemmy's curiosity was baffled, and she
could not quite make up her mind whether
the girl was imposing upon her or not. Beatrice saw that it was useless to remain, for
that no further attempt at any explanation
of Fronica's wishes could be effected, but
she was deeply touched at the effort made
and the risk run by the flower-girl to convey
to her what she felt sure was an important

message; and as the two girls passed through the hall, Beatrice was still more pained to see an expression of despair on the poor girl's face, which she was trying in vain to conceal.

CHAPTER XVII.

Miss Button's Triumphant Success.

DURING their walk home Fronica endeavoured repeatedly to arrest her companion's attention and appeal to her feelings, imploring her by looks and gestures to give back the note she had so rudely seized. But not the slightest impression seemed to be produced; and as soon as they reached home Miss Button ran up stairs and locked herself into her room. There she eagerly opened and spelt over the note. It had no address, no beginning, and no signature, but the few words Miss Button was able to decipher of the foreign cramped handwriting caused the most triumphant surprise, and she uttered, " Well, if this is not as good as a fifty, or perhaps a hundred pound note to me, my name's not Lizzy Button. Now then, where's my best bonnet? If I won't go there at once and see what I can get for keeping his secret!"

Putting on a coquettish little bonnet, trimmed with cerise ribbon and roses, and her best shawl, she hastened stealthily downstairs, got into the street, unperceived as she thought, and walking quickly directed her steps towards Belgravia.

When she had reached Belgrave Square she slackened her pace, took a leisurely survey of one of the largest houses, seeming to hesitate whether she should ring the door-bell or not. It was now dark and no lights visible in any of the windows except in the basement and dining-room floors. "He may be at dinner," she thought, "but more probably dining out. I'll see what kind of servant comes to the door; nothing venture, nothing have;" and with this wise aphorism she pulled the servants' bell.

The door was not opened for some time, but at last a cross-looking footman came and asked rudely what her business might be.

"Is Sir Bevan Desborough at home, and alone?" inquired Miss Button, as she placed her handsome face and figure in the full light of the hall lamp.

The footman looked somewhat appeased, and said more civilly that his master was just gone out to dine.

"At the club, or at a party?"

"That's more than I can say; but if you are very particular to know, I'll ask his valley."

"Could I see him? or would you be sure to give Sir Bevan a message from me? It's of great consequence, and it will be worth your while."

"Never fear but I'll give it as soon as ever he comes home."

"Then you tell him as soon as he comes home the young person that's making Miss Lillyford's wedding-dress has been sent to ask him something very particular about it, and she wants to see him to-morrow morning. What time does he get up generally?"

"Not much before twelve or one, I think," said the footman.

"Well, you can see him to-night when he comes home, and tell him I'll be here between twelve and one; mind that you say it's from Lady Lillyford."

"Yes, I'll do it," said he.

Miss Button emerged from the bright light of the hall into the comparative darkness of the square, pretty well satisfied with the result of her effort.

"He may tell all the servants if he likes," thought she; "but as I made no mystery, and did not tell him not, he is less likely to say anything." At that moment she fancied she saw a small figure hastening away. "Ha!—who is that?" she said half aloud.

"Can Fronica have followed me? Well, she won't get much good out of it, except a scolding from Madame Rosalie;" and she ran on in the hope of reaching home before her, and thus be able to prove that Fronica was out without leave.

CHAPTER XVIII.

Fronica falls among Friends.

IF, instead of returning direct home in order to get her companion punished, Miss Button had followed the little figure she had seen at the door step, she would perhaps have learnt something about another secret which she wished to penetrate. Fronica (for she it was) waited quietly till Miss Button was out of sight, and probably divining the motive which made her run so fast round the corner, shook her head with the mournful hopeless look which her wan features often wore, and then left Belgrave Square by a different street.

She passed up Grosvenor Place, along Piccadilly, and down St. James's Street, then along Pall Mall to St. James's Place. When she had arrived there, she took a piece of paper from her pocket, wrote a few words in pencil, and knocked at one of the doors on the Park side of the street.

It was soon answered, and she held up the paper for the servant to read. He asked if she would wait a minute while he went to inquire if his master could see her, as he was at dinner.

She understood this, and motioned for him to go, while she sat down on a chair in the hall.

In less than a minute the dining-room door opened again. The tall dark gentleman who had excited Clemmy's curiosity came out, and shook the dumb girl warmly by the hand. Then ordering lights to be taken up into the drawing-room, he led her upstairs with the respectful courtesy of the old school.

"Sit down," he said, "and don't be in a hurry. I am only too glad you are able to leave that dingy shop and come here, for I have much to say. But you want to tell me something first, I see."

He gave her pen and ink, and she hastily wrote what had occurred that day, and how she had failed in giving a note to Beatrice, as she wished ardently to have done.

"And one of Madame Rosalie's girls has got it," he said, "and probably has taken it to Sir Bevan Desborough. Ha! that is unlucky, for I did not wish him to be on his guard; but never mind, it can't be helped, and you did it from the best of motives. Don't be alarmed."

But she saw that he was, therefore it was not easy for him to reassure her; and she leaned her head on her hand with a dejected look.

"You are tired; fool that I am to have forgotten to make you take something." He ran down stairs and soon brought up some fruit and wine. "There is only my brother and a friend with me, but I thought you would prefer not to see them or I would have taken you at once into the dining-room to eat something more comfortably. Take courage now, for everything is going on well, I trust; and in a few days the man I sent to Naples to obtain the certificate must arrive, and then we may proceed at once. Never fear, and remember the words you wrote down in your kind effort to reassure Miss Lillyford, saying that she will not have the misery of marrying Sir Bevan, could really do no harm. Unless," he added, as his countenance clouded over, " he should trace them to *you* and endeavour to do *you* some injury. I feel sure you had better leave Madame Rosalie's at once, and go to my Aunt at Langton Hall; she would be only too glad to see you. Do not return there at all—nay, I insist on it. There is no knowing, if his evil passions are excited, what he may not do."

" Yes," he said, in answer to her inquiring eyes, " my brother is going to her this very evening, and he will take charge of you on the railway."

Fronica shook her head, wrote a few words, and showed them to him.

" Nonsense !—a burden to her !—that you could never be, you would only be too useful; you can teach her children to write Italian, make flowers, and a thousand beautiful things."

Fronica's face brightened at this idea, though she tried to make further objections —such as,

" What would Madame Rosalie think ?"

" I will settle it all afterwards with Madame Rosalie—but I would rather not ap-. pear in the matter for some little time yet. It would do the ill-natured girl good if she were to think you had drowned yourself, or had been lost; it is much better they should not be able to discover you till the trial is safely over. In fact, I am quite sure it is quite providential your having come here tonight, for they will never be able to trace you now. Now eat this, and then lie down on the sofa to rest for half an hour. Meantime I will go and tell my brother that he is to take you with him."

He left the room, and Fronica did as she was bid; for there was no mistaking the kindly expression of those benevolent eyes. Moreover, she felt that he was doing what was best both for her and the object they both had at heart. She was so worn out with fatigue and anxiety, that when she laid her weary head on the sofa-cushion, she fell at once into a quiet, child-like sleep.

When the gentlemen came into the room an hour afterwards, Fronica was still asleep, and her innocent face, in its childlike simplicity and purity, shaded by the tresses of dark hair which had fallen from under her bonnet, was one that would have been difficult to look upon unmoved.

" How very handsome she is !" exclaimed the younger of the two.

"I always thought so; but she has suffered so fearfully, poor child!"

"Well, I do not wonder at your taking up her cause so zealously. I only hope all the trouble you have taken will be rewarded with success. I see you must remain in London, for you have plenty on your hands, and I will do my best to take care of this poor child. I'm sure my Aunt will be delighted with her."

"I hope so—in fact, I am sure she will; but it is time to start, and the cab is at the door, and I am afraid we must awake her."

He approached gently, and as his shadow passed over the light, she awoke. Starting up she looked hurriedly round, endeavouring to recollect where she was. Then she saw the kind face bending over her with a look of profound respect.

Putting on her shawl and bonnet hurriedly to rights, she signified that she was ready to start.

CHAPTER XIX.

Sir Bevan Desborough alters his Plans.

THE next day Sir Bevan Desborough called in Portman Square at an earlier hour than usual. Beatrice was sitting near the drawing-room window, writing out her mother's visiting-list for the day. She generally sat near the window, and often looked out into the Square, in the hope of seeing the dark stranger, whose compassionate looks always dwelt pleasantly in her mind.

Since the poor flower-girl's unsuccessful attempt to give her a note on the preceding day, she had hoped that some important news was about to be conveyed to her, and that the stranger was in some way mixed up in it; that it might in some way relate to

Arthur Brookfield was of course her only solution of the mystery.

She was startled from the reverie caused by these vague surmises, by an exclamation from Clemmy and a knock at the hall door.

"What can make Sir Bevan call so much earlier to day?" said Clemmy; "I thought he was always late of a morning."

"I suppose he's coming to luncheon," said Lady Lillyford. "I am afraid we have not a very good one."

But to their surprise he did not come up stairs, and Lady Lillyford found, on inquiring, that he had asked to see Sir Charles very particularly, and had been shown into the library.

"What can it be?" said Clemmy, with a face of alarm, for she had never been quite easy since her failure to ascertain what that mysterious note contained the day before. She had resolved to drive that afternoon to Madame Rosalie herself about it, and inquire who the strange Italian girl was.

Clemmy's anxious looks were not lost on Beatrice, who felt a dawning of hope revive in her mind, knowing well that her marriage with Sir Bevan was the all-important object of Clemmy's wishes, in order to forward her own views and her marriage with Roland.

Clemmy then left the room, and, taught by recent experience, Beatrice felt sure that she was gone to listen at the library door.

She was right in her supposition. The butler, as he afterwards told the housekeeper, was so taken all of a heap by seeing Sir Bevan so flustered and his hands tremble as he put down his hat, that anyone might have knocked him down with a feather, and that he wished to be handy to the library door for fear that anyone might be taken ill.

Whether the feather was to be applied to Sir Bevan or himself he never fully explained, but he thereby justified his proximity to the library, when, as he said, he saw Miss Gubbins coming down stairs like a cat, and knew

what she was after. When Clemmy appeared, he retired, and left her in the undisturbed pleasure of listening. What she
there heard seemed to give her very little
satisfaction, but she did not obtain by any
means as much information as she required,
for soon the door opened, and it was as
much as she could do to get out of the way
and sneak up the back stairs.

Presently she took her usual place in the
drawing-room, and tried to look as composed
as if she had not left it. But Beatrice perceived that she was out of breath, and that
she could scarcely conceal her agitation.

In another minute Sir Bevan's carriage
drove off from the door, and Clemmy exclaimed,

"Why, he's not coming up stairs at
all!"

"I suppose it was some business he had
to settle with Charles—something about Roland, I dare say," said Lady Lillyford, who
was not much given to evil prognostications,

and was rather relieved that Sir Bevan did not remain for luncheon.

Clemmy wanted to make an expedition by herself that afternoon, or at least without Beatrice; but as she and Lady Lillyford had both agreed that Beatrice must never be left by herself, lest she should receive some letter which might upset their plans, she was obliged to persuade Lady Lillyford that she looked tired, and would be all the better for remaining at home, and nurse herself for the dinner-party to which they were all invited.

She was in the act of making this suggestion, when Sir Charles came in, and said he wished to speak to Lady Lillyford in the library.

He looked agitated and annoyed, Beatrice thought, but Lady Lillyford did not perceive it, and only said, " Had we not better have luncheon first ?"

" Oh, hang the luncheon!—I must see you; and, Miss Gubbings, you must go and hasten the dressmakers and tradespeople about your and Beatrice's trousseau, for I find the wedding must take place next week—Saturday at the latest."

He said this in a stern voice, and when he saw Beatrice endeavouring to speak, he waved his hand with a look of command, as if determined not to hear anything she had to say.

"But," urged Clemmy, "surely Roland will not be ready by that time—his business—"

"Will all be done—Sir Bevan has promised it—I will explain it all to Lady Lillyford—or," he added, "to you if you like better:" for it then occurred to him that Clemmy knew best how to manage his daughter.

"With all my heart," said Clemmy—"that is if Lady Lillyford will allow me to know the reason of this change of plan."

"Ah, yes, do,—you know I hate business, and I really am so exhausted. I want my luncheon, and, Beatrice, you look quite pale too—I'm sure you want food."

Clemmy descended with Sir Charles into the library, and endeavoured to extract from him all that Sir Bevan had said, and his reasons for wishing to expedite the wedding.

It seemed a strange story, and she suspected that there was something more that he did not tell. It appeared that Sir Bevan had a letter from Nice that morning, giving a less good account of his sister, who was consumptive, and had gone there for her health; that he wished to see her, yet could not bear the idea of going there without Beatrice, and was most anxious to have the wedding sooner than the time originally proposed.

Sir Charles said that he seemed sadly cut up at the illness of his favourite sister, but when he suggested that it would be better for him to go at once, and return for the wedding, he had answered in a very excited manner, and said that he could not bear the uncertainty as to what might happen to Beatrice while he was away.

"If you can persuade the girl, I don't know that I see any harm in it," added Sir Charles with a look of helpless misery; "but I really can't stand her tears—poor child, I sometimes think it is not right so to force her inclination."

"Nonsense," said Clemmy, "when we know it is for her good—to ensure her a comfortable, luxurious home, and a handsome and agreeable husband."

"But not a good man, I fear; however, it is too late now to think of that, but I can't help suspecting that it is not quite on his sister's account—but that he wants to get away from London for—for some reason or another."

Clemmy wondered in her own mind whether Fronica could in any way be connected with this sudden decision of Sir Bevan's, but yet could not possibly imagine how. Taking these things into consideration, Clemmy thought it was all the more important to go to Madame Rosalie's and try to unravel the mystery.

Unlike Lady Lillyford, Clemmy was too pre-occupied to eat a good luncheon, and having ordered the carriage half an hour sooner, she left Lady Lillyford to the enjoyment of her fricaseed chicken, and Beatrice to play with her knife and fork under the impression that she was eating.

CHAPTER XX.

Does Success bring Happiness?

WHAT a life of expectancy most of us turbulent and wishing mortals lead! We are dissatisfied with the day and the hour, yet feel a confidence which no amount of disappointment can uproot, that if some particular thing would but happen, we should be perfectly happy. And when we have attained the object of our desires—the one thing which we confidently think will turn this world into a paradise—how very few of us, even then, remain long satisfied. Again the day and the hour seem barren of anticipated results. Some still coveted vineyard, some unattainable ewe-lamb soon begins to trouble our joy; some item in the details that make up the condition of our beau-ideal is wanting, so that the two columns of hopes and fulfilments do not balance. Yet, if the success of our ardent desires fails to produce entire happiness, so, on the other hand, does their failure, or even the fulfilment of apprehended misfortunes, fail to produce the entire misery we expected. On the contrary, we are often so evidently supported in misfortune by an unseen power, that our greatest trials sometimes produce a more complete feeling of real peace and hope than the attainment of our ardent wishes.

I was visited by this peace and hope in the one misfortune I had always dreaded most—my mother's death. So I speak from long experience.

"If I could only be freed from this engagement, and knew that Arthur cared for me a little, how happy I should be!" thought Beatrice that day, as she sat in the drawing-room in Portman Square.

In a distant county far away, Elfrida

thought, as she looked out of the window over Oakhampton Park, "If I could only hear that Edward Luscombe was safe, how entirely I should be able to enjoy that lovely view and the glorious spring sunshine."

Elfrida had been reading over again that morning one of the (to her) most interesting portions of Lady Lillyford's diary. And after she had described minutely her baby-boy, knowing well how much Mrs. Somerton would sympathise in all relating to her child, the writer went on to say: "A kind of presentiment at times comes over me that my darling's future life will be one of many crosses and troubles. It may be fanciful, but this idea has gained more possession of me since I have discovered a little mark just like a red cross on his white skin, under his little left shoulder. Ah! dear friend, if his father and I should die, promise me—promise that you will watch over my boy as if he were your own!"

Can the mark be still there?—if Edward

be indeed her son? Elfrida had asked herself repeatedly since reading the above passage. "But, oh! if I could but know that
he were safe, how little would anything else
signify!" was the response her heart had
given to the question.

One of her sources of anxiety was destined
to be cleared up that day, for the postman
brought a letter directed in a handwriting
which made her almost faint with the excitement of mingled fear and joy. It was *his*
writing, she felt sure, but so indistinct and
blurred, it seemed as if he had written it
with his left hand. Mrs. Somerton had not
looked at the letters which were brought in,
but she saw by Elfrida's changing colour
that one of them must be from Edward
Luscombe. The tender-hearted mother went
to the further end of the room, that she
might not see her daughter's face while she
was reading the letter. She wished her to
feel that no eye, not even a mother's, could
see the expression of her features as she

read ; but great was her suspense and consequent joy at Elfrida's half audible "Thank God !" as in a few minutes she went over and threw herself into her mother's arms.

"But—oh! mamma, what a fearful escape he has had ; and look, his writing is scarcely legible, for his right arm was broken, and he was dreadfully bruised from the effects of a fall in the cave. I will tell you what I gather principally from the letter, which is very long, you see."

CHAPTER XXI.

What happened in the Caves of Adelsberg.

" AND poor Dorina, is she safe?" inquired Mrs. Somerton.

" Alas! I cannot make out whether they have heard anything of her—but I will read that part first, where he was still with her. He says:

" ' At the end of the emerald walk there was a deep chasm, and when the cries were heard the Gräfin and I, followed at a distance by some others, proceeded in that direction. Then the lights suddenly went out, I suppose, and in this way we must have got into one of the smaller caverns, for we unexpectedly found ourselves in darkness, and looking round, could see no light in any direction.

" 'What was to to be done? We called as loud as we could, and tried to find our way back, groping towards the opening by which we must have entered this smaller cave. On we walked, as quickly as we could—on, or rather round—calling out at intervals, and feeling by the sides, until I felt the Gräfin's arm, which I hitherto held, slip from my grasp. Then I heard what seemed to be a plunge in some water far below, and a faint cry.

" 'I started down, as I thought, after her. It seemed to be an inclined plane, and there was the sound of a stream running at the bottom. But it was not deep, I thought. I waded about for some time, but could find no trace of her. In vain I called—no answer was returned. Could the current have carried her away? I then followed its course for some distance, wading through the deepest part, where in some places there was a strong stream, almost a torrent, and my fear was that it might already have sucked her down. In some places the top of the cave struck my head, and I had to stoop quite low; at others it seemed as if the cave was high and large. At last I came to a place where the stream seemed to divide, for I distinctly heard it flowing away on my left hand.

" My perplexity was greatly increased, but I thought it better to follow the one which I felt to be the deeper of the two; and after pursuing its course for some distance, I felt the roof getting lower and lower down upon my head, while the waters rose to my breast. Putting my hand forward, I could feel that the water rose as high as the top of the arch, or rather that the passage was so low and narrow, that there was no room to proceed without the certainty of being drowned. So I waded back against the current—but with considerable difficulty, and then followed the other, thinking it might lead to some opening outside the mountain. I had not proceeded very far along the other branch of the stream, when I suddenly fell down into what seemed a bottomless abyss, for during my downward course I seemed filled with recollections of the past—your image was the principal and most distinct object—and all my former life passed in review before me.

" ' Then I felt a blow on my head, and lost all consciousness. How long this lasted I never knew, and probably shall never be able to ascertain, for I have but a dim recollection of suffering, and seeing shadowy and uncouth forms hovering about. Whether these were real persons, or phantoms of delirium, I know not; but I think that kind of state must have lasted many days, and that I was then in the cavern. I think I regained no real consciousness until I saw the sun shining through the crevice of some planks, and felt a whiff of fresh air breathing on my aching forehead. No person was visible. I seemed unable to speak, and I must have sunk to sleep, I believe, for when

I awoke all was dark again, and I heard voices talking and laughing in some distant spot. I could not distinguish any words, and was too weak and ill to feel any curiosity about them. But a burning sensation of thirst induced me to call out, in hopes of getting some water to cool my parched lips. So I called out as loud as I could, and soon afterwards a door opened, and an old woman entered with a light. She was hard-featured, and did not look with much kindness upon me. I asked for water, and she disappeared again without saying anything.

" 'Presently afterwards a light again gleamed through the door-chinks; then a younger woman, but with equally hard features, opened it, and brought me a jug of water. She inquired, with some appearance of kindness, how I felt. She spoke the language of the peasantry, which, fortunately, I understood. Of course I immediately inquired where I was, and how I had been rescued from the cave.

" 'She put her finger on her lips, and whispered low to me that I must not speak—seeming to hint that she did not wish any one to know that I was there.

" 'I found afterwards this was the case. I had been found by a band of smugglers, or rather thieves, who lived on the further side of the Hohenstein range of mountains. The hard-featured young woman was the daughter of one of these, and she had accompanied him on some of his marauding expeditions. It appeared when he found me he thought I was not quite dead, but would do nothing to save or rescue me, lest the secret of his hiding-place in that part of the cavern should become known. But this daughter, being less hard-hearted, induced him to show her the spot where I lay, and had persuaded him to remove me to one of the outer caverns where he kept his stores. There she had attended me (as I afterwards found with great kindness) for several days, and thinking I should regain my reason better if

I were taken out of the cavern into the air, she and her mother had contrived to remove me. But now that I had regained my reason the girl was much alarmed for her father's safety, and endeavoured to express, as well as she was able, the dilemma in which she was placed.

" 'My first effort, before I could move at all, was to induce her to give me writing materials, that I might communicate with you and other friends.

" 'But this she resolutely refused. She said it would bring the authorities upon them, and her father would certainly be arrested. But she promised that if I followed her orders I should soon be well enough to leave the place, and then she trusted that gratitude to her for having saved my life would prevent me from betraying her father and his gang of thieves.

" ' Of course they had taken my purse and my watch, and other things I had about me. My rough attendant proved herself a good doctor, and had contrived to set my arm when she discovered it was broken.

" 'I am now writing with my left hand. As soon as I felt strong enough to walk a few miles I set off from the cave. I am now writing from the first village I have come to, and as I am anxious to arrive in England, I shall write to Hohenstein for my things, and beg to know whether they have had any tidings of the poor Gräfin. Of course the party has been broken up, and therefore I do not like to go back. If they have heard nothing of her, I fear she must have met with a fate similar to mine, and fallen into one of those awful chasms which so nearly cost me my life. I shall wait here, as I am almost done up, and besides have no money to pay for my bed and board, until the peasant whom I have sent with a note to Gratz shall return.' "

They read the letter several times over, talking and commenting upon it together, for some time.

CHAPTER XXII.

More Good News.

WHEN the paroxysms of joy and thankfulness were somewhat subdued, which in Elfrida were so great as to prove most exhausting to her frail health (for joy does kill more easily than grief), they remembered how gratifying the news would be to the Mordaunts and Mr. Fairleigh.

Therefore they walked to the Rectory, and Elfrida, in the full consciousness of a positive engagement, no longer shrank from the mention of Edward Luscombe's name.

To their surprise they found the Mordaunts already in a state of excitement as great, though not so painful, as on the memorable day when they received the news of the catastrophe which had caused so much sorrow.

They were both so pre-occupied, that they were scarcely able to take in the good news brought by the Somertons. Even a greater joy, mingled with some drops of nervous anxiety, was visible on Mr. Mordaunt's face, while Peggy's broad cheeks shone forth in the full exuberance of unmingled delight.

"I knew it was so; I was sure of it all along, but I never would say a word—never," exclaimed Peggy.

"You mean that you were sure that Edward was not guilty of running off with the heiress, and that he never ceased to care for Elfrida?"

"Yes, I thought that too; but this is better, far better, for everybody."

"But it is not sure yet—and I fear very improbable," interrupted her brother.

"Oh! but it will, it must—besides it will be so easily ascertained," said Peggy, "now they have got a clue. You know that it is possible to ascertain whether he has the very mark—the cross under the left shoulder. How providential it was that you had that dream to point out to you where the old journal was!"

"But a great deal must be proved," said Mr. Mordaunt; "and remember the law is so uncertain."

"Hang the law!" said Peggy; "what do I care for the law, if it can be proved that Edward Luscombe, who is the very image of his mother—of that beautiful Lady Lillyford—is indeed her son. That dream was sent from heaven. I know it was, to help to confirm the discovery; and now to think of Lady Horatia having fished out the old mad woman who can prove it all. And he will have that place and title and fortune, and the poor old trees won't be cut down, after all; and that extravagant gambler will never be Sir Roland . . . and that pert minx who gives herself such airs, I know, to dear Mrs. Dronington and all those people who were worth anything—to think how delightfully taken in she will be! Why, the two weddings are to be next Saturday, —Sir Bevan Desborough has hastened them —and—and . . . But you must not say a word about it, it is all a secret yet—and nothing prepared.   Oh! I could cry with delight!"

"But what has happened, dear Peggy?" said Mrs. Sómerton, half bewildered; "you are only telling us the end—what has given rise to all this . . . this surmise—for I suppose it is scarcely more?"

"Surmise—no, indeed, it's more than that. There's Mr. Fairleigh been telegraphed for by Mr. Sterndale, and Miss Rosa has just been telling us a great deal (but it is all a secret yet, you know; only I thought you and Elfrida ought to hear as much as we know), and they suspect a great deal more, and think that something will be discovered which may have the effect of preventing poor Miss Lillyford's marriage with that worthless Sir Bevan; but I really could hardly take that in, I was so full of asking them more questions than they could possibly answer about Edward Luscombe. And really I'm quite out of breath with it all," continued Peggy, wiping her forehead, for the day was warm and her excitement was great. "And," added she after a pause, "they find now that wretched woman Rachel Harraway is alive, and Mr. Sterndale has telegraphed to Mr. Fairleigh to meet him at York, where they think they have ascertained she is still living in a small back street. Mr. Sterndale met Lady Horatia, and she has stirred him up to do all this for poor Edward Luscombe's sake."

"Unless Rachel will confess—and how could she be made to confess that she burnt her own child?" said Mrs. Somerton, with a shudder; "I do not see how it could ever be possible to prove it. However, if we find that Edward has that mark under the shoulder mentioned (in the diary which we found) by my darling Matilda, I shall be quite satisfied, and I am sure Elfrida will not care whether it is legally proved or not —I am sure she would not wish to deprive the parents of her friend Beatrice of fortune and position."

"Oh, no!" exclaimed Elfrida. "That he is not the son of that wicked woman is all he or I would require to know, and I feel already sure of it."

"I hope so," said Peggy; "but I must say that depriving the owners is no deprivation at all, for of course Sir Edward would never have left it away if he had known his own legitimate son was alive. Besides, it serves them quite right. What is the good of a country place to them, I should like to know? Why, they might just as well have been living in the moon for any good it was to them, or they to it! Lady Lillyford did nothing but complain, and snub all the neighbours; and it would have broken our hearts and all the poor people's to see that poor reckless Roland playing ducks and drakes with everything, and that pert minx Miss Gubbings the lady of the Hall. And really I, for one, cannot help being glad to think how she will be taken in, for she quarrelled with her sister and Lady Horatia Nolan, and now she will never be Lady Lillyford, after all. How Roland, with all his faults, could have fallen in love with her, I can't think, for she certainly is not everybody's money, to my mind."

"Still three thousand a year, or more, you know," said Mr. Mordaunt.

"Yes, but she will take it out in worry, see if she does not. He will find her dear at the money," said Peggy. "You know I am one of those who say his faults are not exactly a part of his nature—he fell into bad hands."

"And what is this about Sir Bevan Desborough?" inquired Mrs. Somerton.

"Well, they did not know anything positive, and their brother was in such a hurry to be off after the letters came in, that they did not quite hear what Mr. Sterndale said in his letter, except that he thought poor Miss Lillyford would die, she is looking so dreadfully ill and thin, the shadow of what she was two months ago. So Rosa is in great anxiety, for every reason, that Miss Lillyford should be freed from her engagement; for although the sisters dare not mention the subject to their brother, they hope he will in time be convinced (as Rosa is) that Beatrice cares for him. They are so anxious for him to marry her, for they tell me he is quite heart-broken—entirely an altered man, and seems to take no interest in anything."

CHAPTER XXIII.

Clemmy Gubbings endeavours to outwit Miss Button.

WHEN Miss Clementina Gubbings arrived at Madame Rosalie's, instead of going into the shop, she asked to be shown into a private room.

"Madame Rosalie went to Paris yesterday morning," was the answer; "but if you like to see Miss Simpkinson, she is the person as everything is left in charge."

Yes, Clemmy would like to see Miss Simpkinson.

She was shown into a comfortable-looking back parlour, and after waiting a few minutes, a tall thin woman appeared, whose dress did not do credit to her professional powers, nor her contour to the prosperity of the business. Clemmy thought she had seldom seen a more uncomfortable and woebegone-looking individual. She was evidently in a great state of flurry and embarrassment, but whether it was her normal condition, or caused by some present misfortune, Clemmy could not quite make up her mind. It was soon cleared up, however, by Miss Simpkinson's own words.

" Oh! dear, ma'am, I'm sure it's a wonder I'm alive. I don't know what your ladyship wants to see me about, but I'm sure, after not sleeping a wink last night, and all I've gone through since Madame Rosalie has left, it's a wonder if I have any sense left."

Clemmy did not think she appeared as if she had much at any time.

" The fact is, ma'am, a dreadful thing has happened—one of our young ladies—(and for the matter of that they are always doing something to aggravate one)—there was Miss Muggins only last week——"

"But what has happened?" said Clemmy, who was beginning to get impatient at the doings in the shop.

"It's the Italian girl, ma'am; and I said to Madame Rosalie, when she consulted me about her, that it does not do to take people one does not know, though her flowers have made that department of our business quite celebrated; and she looked indeed very ladylike—still, she had no recommendation from people we knew, and so I said there was no knowing what might happen. And now to think it has just occurred, as I said, while Madame is absent, and as I before said, that such responsibility, and all those young people on my hands——"

"What has happened?"

"She has fled, ma'am!—went out last night and never returned, and I sat up all night expecting, and no news of her at all!"

"Does not Miss Button know?"

"Ah! there again—the trouble I have had with that Miss Button no tongue can tell—such a temper!—such tantrums! I am sure no one that wasn't born a lady, as I was, could ever have put up with her doings—but it's because I was reduced. I that never put a pin into myself till my father failed—never so much as dressed my own hair."

"But the—the Italian, do tell me what became of her?"

"Why, mum, that's just what we all want to know."

"Has she eloped?"

"Oh! I think not; she was very well conducted for a foreigner, I must say."

"But surely Miss Button—you know, they were both with us yesterday, and I think they quarrelled."

"Oh! very likely."

Miss Simpkinson placed her hand on her forehead with a theatrical air, as if meditating profoundly, and then said, " Will you be pleased to see Miss Button yourself, for I can't make head or tail of her. One moment she protests she knows nothing, and then she bursts out crying; and I do think she knows more about the poor girl than she chooses to say."

" Let me see her," said Clemmy; " and I should like to have her alone."

" Well," said Miss Simpkinson, drawing herself up, " if *you* please," as if she were not quite sure whether she was keeping up her dignity sufficiently by consenting to this arrangement.

Miss Simpkinson left the room, and presently Miss Button came in. Clemmy was struck with the alteration in her appearance since the preceding day. There was considerably less pride and insolence in her face, and traces of tears were plainly seen.

" I wish you would tell me the truth," said Clemmy. " What has become of the Italian girl ?"

" I really don't know," said she, bursting into tears—" I'd give—yes, a 'fifty pound note, I would, if anybody would shew her to me alive and well. I do fear—for we had a quarrel, and I am really sorry for it, I am, indeed. I never wished to do her harm, I really didn't."

" But what did you do to her ?—and why would you not show me the note she wanted to give to Miss Lillyford?"

" I—I—thought to make something by it —and——"

" What have you done with it ? Taken it to Sir Bevan Desborough, I suppose. Tell me the truth. I know you did; and what was it about ?"

Miss Button gave no answer, but began to sob violently, and then stammered out—

" It's very hard, indeed it is! I'm sure I didn't mean to do any mischief indeed."

" Never mind what you meant to do, only tell me the plain truth. What was in that note, and what have you done with it?"

"I—I——"

"Well, tell me at once, or I will complain of you to Madame Rosalie. I'll tell her how impertinent you were in forcing that note away from me."

"But it was not addressed to you, mum," said Miss Button, becoming herself again for a moment.

"That's no excuse, for you could not prove it was not—besides, you snatched it out of Miss Lillyford's hand, and that was equally impertinent."

"Oh! ma'am, just as if I didn't know that you wanted her not to get it! If you turn against me now, when I was trying to help."

"If you will shew me the note I won't turn against you. Remember that it is for Miss Lillyford's good—we wish to guard her from harm," said Clemmy, with a conscious look of what is often called "proper pride."

"Really, mum, I don't know what to do

or say. I only wish I had let that poor girl
alone, who never did me any harm ; and I
won't make any more mischief, that I
won't."

"What harm can it do now to tell me,
I should like to know? On the contrary,
if you really wish to know what has become
of her, I might be able to help you, if you
give me some clue. Where did you see the
girl last ?" asked Clemmy, for she found that
the only chance of coming to the truth was
by working on the hard and haughty-look-
ing girl's sudden and most unexpected soft-
ness of heart. "Where, and when ?—answer
me truly. I may really be able to help
to her discovery."

"It was half-way down Halkin Street,
when I was coming back from Belgrave
Square, that I lost sight of her poor tearful
face. I would not speak to her, for I was
provoked, and wanted to get home first."

"You had been at Sir Bevan Desborough's house, then ? I am sure you had."

Miss Button drew herself up with a touch of her usual arrogance, and said,

"Well, and what if I was? I was not doing any harm."

"I don't care about that—but I can see you gave him the note, and you made him pay you well for it."

"If I did, then, I'm sure I'd give it all up if I could but know that poor girl was safe somewhere."

A bright idea seemed to strike Clemmy, and after a few minutes' consideration she said,

"Well, now, I've thought of a plan by which you really could ascertain what has become of her. You must surely remember a tall dark gentleman who was talking to her one day, and gave her a paper to read? Ah! I see you do. Well, it's plain that he knows who she is, and probably she may have taken 'refuge with him. Now, I believe you make dresses for Lady Horatia Nolan. Ah! I thought so. Well, that gentleman is acquainted with her, or, at least, he went to visit her one day, for I saw him standing at the door, and I believe he was let in. You can easily make an excuse to go there, and describe him to the servant, and find out what his name is."

Miss Button's face brightened, and her proud spirit and love of intrigue seemed to revive at the thought.

" I see you understand it," said Clemmy; " go as soon as you can, and then come and tell me the result. I shall be home by six o'clock, so mind that you be there by that time."

" If you'll please to say a word to Miss Simpkinson, ma'am, 'cause she's dreadful perticler, and after what has happened about Fronica, it's as much as our lives are worth to get out without orders. So please tell her that you want me directly to do something for you at your house."

" Yes, and I was nearly forgetting the chief object of my visit here—it is to hasten the dresses as much as possible, because the marriage—both marriages are to take place sooner than was intended. So they must all be ready by Tuesday at latest." Then Clemmy added with a smile, for she wished to keep Miss Button in good humour now, " I feel sure it is your doing. Something in that note you gave to Sir Bevan Desborough has made him do this; so if you have to work all the harder to get them ready, it is your own fault. I can't see there's much harm in that, though, as far as it goes, so you need not mind that."

But Miss Button did see harm in it, for she had noticed how very ill and unhappy Beatrice looked, and to her newly-troubled conscience it seemed a pity that a marriage should take place between that good and gentle-looking Miss Lillyford and so questionable a man as Sir Bevan. Whether this active state of conscientiousness was dependent on anything more than the impulse of her better feelings with regard to Fronica's uncertain fate, may reasonably be doubted, but it certainly influenced her now, and aroused in her an earnest desire to find out what she could regarding the fate of Fronica.

Clemmy then went up into the show-room to choose some flowers and trimmings, which were to be sent to her house at once by Miss Button, to whom she would give further orders when she got home. Miss Simpkinson was to be sure to see that all the things were forwarded as soon as possible, and Clemmy added in a lower tone to that trembling lady,

"I am quite satisfied with Miss Button's explanation of what has occurred."

"I am very glad, ma'am, I am sure," said Miss Simpkinson, as she followed Miss Gubbings down to the street-door—"very glad to find you are satisfied; but I can't say I am, for I suppose, if the poor girl is found, there will be an inquest, and all sort of dreadful things, and the papers will take it up, and say it was because of the cruelty she met with in this first-rate establishment, than which nothing can be farther from the facts of——"

"Oh! I hope not; besides, I feel *quite sure* she will soon turn up all right somewhere. I daresay she met some friends who took her home. You'll be sure to hear soon."

"Well, I hope your ladyship—miss, I mean—is right."

But Miss Simpkinson looked as if all hope of anything ever going right in this world had lost its expression on her woe-begone countenance.

CHAPTER XXIV.

Will the plan succeed?

CLEMMY went afterwards to make the visits and leave the cards, as she had promised Lady Lillyford she would do, when she persuaded her to remain at home and rest well for the dinner-party. It was a little past six when she got home—and Clemmy hoped to hear that Miss Button was waiting for her in her room. In this she was not disappointed. So she ran upstairs without going into the drawing-room, saying she would not keep the girl waiting any longer.

" Well, you've found out something, I see by your face !" she said, after carefully seeing that the door was closed.

"Not much, I am afraid. I had a hard matter to get Lady Horatia's servants to remember; but one of them thought the name was Sterndale."

"Has he been there often?"

"I believe not, as far as they could remember, only two or three times."

"Sterndale! Let's look at the Court Guide. I'll go down for it."

Clemmy ran down to the drawing-room, and, to pacify Lady Lillyford, who was exceedingly cross and tired of sitting at home, said,

"In one minute I'll be back; but I wanted Miss Button to call with some flowers on an old friend, and I forget her number, so I must run up with this. I'll be back directly." "R, S, St, Ste," murmured Clemmy, as she turned over the leaves while she was running upstairs. "Here it is. Sterndale, Henry, Lincoln's Inn Fields. Sterndale, Norfolk Villa, Camden Town. James Sterndale, 19 Baker Street. Sterndale,

John, St. James's Place. That's the most likely street for an acquaintance of Lady Horatia's," thought the sapient Clemmy, as she showed the page to Miss Button. "Now, could you not make some excuse to call there? I'll tell you. Go knock at the door, and ask for Mrs. Smith, and say you want most particularly to see her about a friend of yours, who you think called there last evening. Say all this before the servant has time to tell you that no Mrs. Smith lives there, and you will soon see by his face whether the girl did come. If not, you might inquire at the other Sterndale's."

"Yes, I see, ma'am. I'll try; but, you see, all this will take up my time."

"Never mind, you shall be well paid, for I am more anxious than ever now to hear who and what that man is, and to ascertain the girl's fate. Don't you see it's the only clue you have to finding out whether she is safe or not. Stay a moment, I'll ask Miss Lillyford, she may give me a clue as to which Sterndale it is likely to be, if she has ever heard the name."

So she went into Beatrice's room—which was next her own—and having again closed the door between the two rooms, said, in her most conciliating manner,

"Trixey, darling, did you ever know or hear of a Mr. Sterndale?"

Beatrice considered for a moment, having learnt caution during those last miserable weeks, and, moreover, having made the painful discovery that Clemmy was treating her with great cruelty.

"Think well, darling, because I fancy he may be a friend of yours; or if not, of some one you once cared for."

Beatrice blushed with the nearest approach to anger that her kindly nature was capable of feeling, for she could not bear that Clemmy should touch upon that, to her, sacred subject, of her true and great love. Still, she thought, if it might by any possibility lead to some explanation

of Arthur's apparent desertion of her, she
had better at all events try to discover
what Clemmy knew about him.

"I think you knew, or have heard the
name," continued Clemmy; "and it is really
an object now that I should find out about
him."

"Why—what object?" asked Beatrice.

Clemmy was puzzled, but after a moment
she said,

"Because you yourself seemed anxious to
know who that stranger was in Madame
Rosalie's shop, and whom we afterwards
met in the Square."

"Is that Mr. Sterndale?" exclaimed Beatrice, unable to conceal a look of sudden
hope that illumined her beautiful eyes.

"I believe so.   Then you do know who
he is?"

"I have heard the name," said Beatrice
with another tell-tale blush.

"I see; he is perhaps the friend a certain
person travelled with in the East.   There

now—thank you, darling. Go and tell your mamma I am coming to relate all the gossip Mrs. Winchfield told me. Stay, have you any idea whether Mr. Sterndale lives in St. James's Place?"

"I never heard where he lived," said Beatrice with a wearied look; and she went downstairs to her mother.

Clemmy ran back to her own room, and said to Miss Button,

"St. James's Place is the most likely, so try there first; and you might say that the deaf and dumb girl you are anxious about was seen talking to a tall gentleman—you know you can describe him—and you'll see by the servant's face whether that fits his master or not."

Miss Button said she would do the best she could. "But," she added, "Miss Gubbings, you must please to make some good excuse to Miss Simpkinson, in case I am detained, and not able to return home till late in the day. Because," added Miss

Button with a sudden flash of mingled tri-
umph and hope in her large eyes—"because if I can't succeed in finding out anything from the servants, then—I know a—a
person who wouldn't mind running all over
London to do me a good turn. But he
lives a long way off, and I should have to
go to-morrow morning into the City—and
then perhaps not come upon him at once."

Clemmy saw that the artful girl meant to
make a holiday and have some fun; but as
that was no concern of hers, she said, smil-
ing inwardly,

"Well, then, you say to Miss Simpkinson
that you must come to me at nine o'clock
to-morrow morning, and that you will be
wanted to stay here some time to alter the
trimmings and the skirt of the mauve dress."

So Miss Button departed in a more cheerful frame of mind, and felt sure that with
the united efforts of herself and Will Marker
—that most knowing of chaps—she would
be sure to find out what had become of the

poor girl whose mysterious grief had excited the latent spark of kindness that smouldered in a small corner of her heart.

After leaving Portman Square that evening, Miss Button went straight to the number indicated in St. James's Place, and putting on her most demure expression, knocked meekly at the door.

It was answered by the same civil servant who had ushered in Fronica the night before, and Miss Button at once begged, with a tearful face and earnest look, to be allowed to see Mrs. Smith, because she was so very anxious about a friend, who she thought meant to come there the night before, and who, from being deaf and dumb, was really unfit to take care of herself, and might have gone to the wrong house.

"There was a poor girl came here last night," said he, "when they were at dinner, but no Mrs. Smith lives here."

"No, but my poor friend thought she did, I know, and I wasn't sure—so I sat up all night waiting for her; knowing she could not speak or hear, I feared she might have made a mistake and got lost."

"Will you see my master, Mr. Sterndale? Perhaps he can tell you all you want to know."

"Oh! don't trouble him; if you know where she went, that's quite enough."

"Well, I heard that she was going with Mr. Henry to his aunt's place—that's Langton Hall, near Langton Bridge."

"And she went there last night? Oh! thank you—that is quite enough; all I wanted to know was whether she was safe—Thank you; pray do not interrupt your master, for that is all I want to know."

And without leaving the servant time to reply, she walked quickly away and went home. It was too late to do any more now she thought, but intended to go early the next morning, and get Will Marker to find out more. She knew he would have no objection to this kind of job. And although the servant looked civil, and as if he had belonged to a respectable family, yet, as it happened that she had been more accustomed to see the bad than good in human nature, she was not at all satisfied with the intelligence that Fronica was said to have been taken into the country by Mr. Henry Sterndale.

CHAPTER XXV.

Miss Button's Visit to the poor City Work-girl.

ABOUT half-past seven the next morning, Miss Button left home, ostensibly to go to Miss Gubbings in Portman Square, but in reality to find out Will Marker. She walked quickly until she reached Piccadilly, where she got into an omnibus, and went to the City. She did not expect to find the said Will Marker at home, but hoped that the sister with whom he lived would be able to tell her where he was likely to be found.

Mary Marker, who took in plain work, lived in a dingy room of a narrow street, where a very scanty amount of sky could be discovered. But she was a devoted sister.

Only a few years older than Will, she had, ever since the death of their parents, devoted her whole energy to his well-being. She worked and thought for him, and preached to him in her simple and well-meaning, but not very effective way; for he was as wild and reckless, as she was thoughful and thrifty. With considerably more talent and cleverness than she possessed, he had been successful at first in most of his undertakings; but as he had no perseverance, and a decided turn for spending as quickly as possible all his earnings, he would often have been left to starve, or steal, had not her foresight and industry enabled her to lay by a little store for their evil days.

Will Marker was one of the not unfrequent instances of a country lad spoiled by the moral atmosphere of London, as it is breathed by what may be called the outsiders of their class—men who are ready to do anything, but, through the deficiency of some quality or other, take root in nothing. He had been successively a policeman, a supernumerary at a theatre, a waiter at a ham and beef shop, a billiard-marker, and a clerk to a bubble company. He was now without employment, and it was what is popularly termed a "toss up" how he would turn out. In more Christian language, it was a perilous turning-point in his life; for he was intelligent and thoughtless. His early chances had been on the whole bad, and his present associates were questionable.

"If he would but marry some good girl," thought his sister, "it would be the saving of him, for he *has* a heart." This she often said and repeated over and over again, " He *has* a heart," as if to assure herself of a fact which other people often doubted, and which his goings on did not seem to indicate. The Markers had known Lizzie Button in the village where they had lived, before their parents died (a little hamlet about a mile from Langton Bridge), and though the steady Mary Marker often shook her head at the

giddy little Button, still she loved the wayward, clever girl with an elder sister's affection.

Lizzy had risen in the world since then,
chiefly by her own cleverness, and was now
considered to be in a fair way of doing very
well as a dress-maker; for she had a high
post in the great Madame Rosalie's establishment. Moreover, she kept up the acquaintance with her former friends, and never
grew proud towards them, though she did
hold her head very high to most others, they
knew.

So Mary often made the best of Will
Marker's doings, and glossed over his delin-
quencies, when they met, and it was quite a
little gleam of sunshine for the poor, plain,
hard worker when Lizzy wended her way
up their dark narrow stairs, and into her
small dingy room.

When Lizzy Button entered the Markers'
room, on the morning after that visit to Mr.
Sterndale's house (according to the arrange-

ment she had made with Clemmy), she found Mary in a more than usually desponding state. She had caught a cold in her eyes; she felt that she ought not to use them, and yet to pause in her work was to starve, more particularly as Will had got into a scrape and lost all his earnings.

She was trying vainly to thread her needle near the window, when she heard a light, quick step on the stairs, and Lizzy's bright yet anxious face appeared at the door.

"Dear good Mary," said she, "tell me quick where I can find Will. I want to see him on some very particular business."

"Oh, do sit down a bit, dear Lizzy, for I am very sad and troubled with my eyes."

"Oh, don't take it so to heart," said Miss Button. "Rest your eyes, and don't work anymore until they're well. I'll get some lotion for them, that I will, and bring it back with me. I know of some that did one of our girls' eyes good. But where's Will?"

"Will, Lizzy? I am almost afraid to say where I think he is. Let's see, what o'clock is it? for I don't like the place nor the play-mates for him, that I don't. About eight or half-past, I suppose. Well, he talked of going the first thing to inquire about some situation. I didn't rightly understand what, but I know the street, he told me that; I daresay you would meet him as he comes back, if you go directly."

"Well, I'll go and see if I can't give him a little commission to do, that will take him away for a few hours, at all events, or per-haps more."

"Well, I know you won't set him to any-thing wrong, so I hope it will be all for the best, and you come and see me for a bit afterwards."

"Yes, or, better still, it would do your eyes good to come out in the air, and as you can't go on with your work, you may as well get a whiff of the fresh breezes. And you can help to take care of me, you know," added Miss Button, with an arch look.

As they were walking along, they met Will Marker coming towards home. Miss Button lost not a moment in explaining to him her errand, and he professed himself delighted to undertake any commission for her. Moreover, she could afford to promise that she could make it worth his while, for she had received a considerable sum from Sir Bevan Desborough for the intelligence she now regretted having given him; and besides, she intended to make Clemmy refund whatever she should spend. But not a word did she say of this to Will, who thought it was her fair earnings that enabled her to be so lavish in her expenditure. He was to go at once by the train to Langton Bridge, and ascertain whether the deaf and dumb girl, whose appearance she described, had come there, and what she was doing, and in what capacity she was employed, and what reason they had for taking her there.

Langton Bridge was not more than half an hour's journey from London by rail, but she told him he might remain there, if necessary, all that day, and even the next, if he found a difficulty in ascertaining what she wished to know. So he called the first Hansom he could find, and drove off, in hopes of catching the next train. They watched until he had disappeared round the corner, and then turned back towards Mary's house.

Now, if Miss Button could have followed the Hansom cab, and seen what occurred in the next street, she would have been very much annoyed; for the cab was hailed by the very person from whom she would have most desired to keep the secret of the deaf and dumb girl's whereabouts. It was Sir Bevan Desborough himself, who knew the sharp Will Marker well, and had once before employed him on a job of his own, not very creditable to either the payer or the paid.

The cabman pulled up, Will Marker jumped out, while Sir Bevan motioned to him to follow him down a neighbouring street. Arrived there, Sir Bevan gave him lengthened and very particular instructions, to which Will responded by a knowing shake of his head, and a partial closing of one eye. Then the former, dismissing Will with a motion of his hand, and a handsome instalment of the sum promised when the said instructions should have been carried out, walked away, looking unconscious of having any concern with anything or anybody in that locality.

Will Marker bounded back to his cab, desired the driver to take him with all possible speed to E. W. terminus, and lighting a penny cheroot, composed himself in a corner of the Hansom, to reflect profoundly on the best means of carrying out his instructions. The result of these reflections he embodied in the following terse remark, " Well, I'm blessed !"

Soon afterwards Miss Button was walking homewards as fast as she could, with her veil well down.

CHAPTER XXVI.

Clemmy Gubbings' Triumphs over her Sister Meely.

"OH! ho!" suddenly exclaimed Miss Clemmy Gubbings, as she sat at the breakfast-table in Portman Square the following morning, and took up the *Morning Post.* "Ah! well, now, I can't help being glad, for she really deserves it."

"What has happened?" inquired Lady Lillyford, peevishly. "You should not call out so loud—you quite startle me; you forget I'm not at all well this morning."

"Beg pardon; but it really is such fun. Look here at this paragraph in the paper about Meely; and I'm sure it's not my fault, for I always said that Prince Scoragoff

was no more a prince than I am. He tried
me first at Ems, and when he saw I suspected
he was an impostor, he took up with Meely,
and she made herself quite a goose about
him, and I really was frightened out of my
wits for fear she should marry him, till luckily
there came that rich widow, Mrs. Dawkins.
You met her, Lady Lillyford ?"

" Yes—a vulgar, impertinent woman."

" Well, the prince heard all kinds of ex-
aggerated reports of her riches, which I did
my best to confirm, for I didn't like poor
Meely to be so thrown away. But now that
she has behaved so dreadfully to me, I can't
bring myself to feel so very sorry. And
Meely did not really care for him, only she
liked the title, and thought it would be a
good thing to be a princess. He is a sharper,
too, I am certain, and was always at the
gaming-tables."

" Oh ! how very dreadful !" said Beatrice ;
"and is she really going to marry him
now ?"

"So the paper says. Look here: 'We have reason to know that a matrimonial alliance is about to take place between Prince Scoragoff and the beautiful and wealthy Miss Gubbings.' So no doubt Lady Horatia has made it up. Well, to be sure; and then some day he will turn out to be some low fellow—an apprentice to some shoemaker or pastry-cook."

"Oh! how very sad; I wonder you can feel glad to think your sister will be so taken in," said Beatrice, with a gentle but reproachful look.

"Oh! I daresay it's all right," said Sir Charles; "for if he is a Russian, he will be sure to be known at the embassy."

"Oh! but I think he pretended to be a Pole or Hungarian, or something of that sort.—Oh! a young person from Madame Rosalie's, is it?" This last remark was made to the servant, who entered at that moment. "And, there, I haven't half done my breakfast," she added, in an aggrieved tone, but with secret gratification, in hopes that it was Miss Button with some news.

In this hope she was destined to be disappointed, for after gulping down her tea and taking an unfinished bit of toast in her hand upstairs, she found another girl, who had brought some of the dresses to be fitted on, but with only a message from Miss Button, to say she was so very unwell with a sprained ankle she could not leave the house.

"Oh! then, you may wait a little, for I was in the middle of my breakfast; and I hate my dresses being tried on by a different person. I only hurried up not to waste Miss Button's time."

Then Clemmy hastened downstairs again to eat another egg, and have some more hot tea. She found both Sir Charles and his wife bitterly reproaching Beatrice for not eating any breakfast, and they appealed to Clemmy to try and persuade her. In vain she protested that she was very ill, that she could not really taste any food, and that she felt so faint when she got up in the morning, she could scarcely stand.

"Oh! if you would but let me see grandmamma," moaned the poor child, in the midst of her quiet sobs—"oh! pray do; for —for I feel I must die soon—and I do hope I may. It's very wicked, I know, but I can't help it."

"She is starving herself to death," said Lady Lillyford; "and it really is so hard upon us—who are doing everything we can to make her happy! And you *can* swallow, I'm sure you can," she added, holding some strong coffee to Beatrice's lips.

Beatrice tried to drink it, but sank back in her chair, looking so dreadfully pale that Sir Charles, who had seldom looked at her at all lately, was horrified at the change, and he whispered to his wife,

"We had better send for a doctor. Let me see, who is there?"

"Ah! I don't know; but I suppose Dr. Pillcox—he attends mamma, I know. But

I think there is nothing the matter—only she is so out of spirits and out of sorts with everything."

But they could not help seeing that Beatrice was really ill, for since she heard the wedding was to be sooner, her strength had perceptibly failed.

Sir Charles felt more alarmed than his wife, for he probably had a juster idea of the cause of her depression; but as he had also a strong conviction of the necessity of the sacrifice, he had hitherto steeled · his heart against all her appeals, and contrived to shut his eyes to her sufferings. But he now insisted on sending for Dr. Pillcox, for, in his indolent and wrong-headed kind of way, he loved his daughter probably better than he did any one else.

CHAPTER XXVII.

Dr. Pillcox is sent for to attend Beatrice; but Clemmy thinks " It's all nonsense."

I T'S all nonsense," said Clemmy, as she and Lady Lillyford took poor Beatrice upstairs, and put her into an easy-chair in the drawing-room. Then Clemmy remembered that the dressmaker was waiting upstairs, and she said, "Well, I suppose they must do the best they can with the dresses, for dear Trixey will not be able to try them on now, I suppose?"

Beatrice shuddered at the idea, and begged piteously to be allowed to remain where she was.

"So you shall, darling," said Clemmy; "and you know we are so much the same height that I am sure they will be able to do them very well. And I will victimize myself for you—so sit quiet, and try to go to sleep, there's a dear."

" But Beatrice of course could not sleep, although she had scarcely closed her eyes for the last two nights; and she was now in that kind of nervously excited state that she seemed to be constantly haunted with the image of Sir Bevan. His large, highly coloured face, and his insolently passionate glances seemed ever present, and came between her and every person or object she looked at. She seemed to have lost all perception of time.

It might have been minutes or hours that she had sat in that chair, for no distinct impression was felt by her from the moment when Clemmy said she would try on the dresses for her, till her hand was taken hold of, and her pulse felt by an elderly man. Then she heard her mother say,

" I don't think she is really ill—I believe it's half fancy."

Dr. Pillcox's sedate countenance gave no indication of his thoughts, nor did Lady Lillyford look at it, for she was not anxious about her daughter. But Sir Charles was, and on hearing that the doctor was there, he came upstairs, and looked inquiringly in his face.

"Nothing much the matter, is there, doctor?" he inquired, after waiting a few minutes while Dr. Pillcox asked Beatrice some questions as to what she felt.

"I hope not," was the cautious answer. "Derangement of the nervous system. She will require some sedatives and slight tonics, and perfect rest from all excitement—that is absolutely necessary."

"Oh!—oh!—yes—I suppose," said Sir Charles; "but—will you come downstairs with me when you have done speaking to her, and have written the prescription?"

"What do you mean by perfect rest, and no excitement?" inquired Sir Charles, when they had gone downstairs. "You know she is engaged to be married the day after to-morrow."

"Ha! indeed, so soon? Well, we shall see how she is to-morrow, after taking the medicine; but unless she is able to sleep to-night, it may prove a bad case. There is considerable irritation of the brain, and the nerves are sensibly affected. She is likely to see and be haunted by unreal forms."

"Is it dangerous?"

"That entirely depends upon the turn it takes during the next few hours. Unless she can be kept entirely free from all excitement, brain-fever is most likely to ensue."

"Brain-fever! Oh! God forbid! Why, that is most dangerous!"

"Quite so, and therefore she must be kept very quiet, and if there be any subject or person which she dislikes, it or they ought not to be mentioned in her presence."

"How on earth is this to be done, for who can tell what foolish dislikes a young girl may not take it into her head to harbour?"

Dr. Pillcox shrugged his shoulders, as much as to say he could not control the emotions of the mind, he could only see, and, if possible, avert their bad effects on the human frame.   All this he intended the shrug to express, and also that he feared it was a critical case, for it seemed to him that the parents were too sanguine about their daughter.   So he added,

"You had better have the prescription made up at once, and see that it is given directly, and I will call again this evening. Good day."

CHAPTER XXVIII.

Sir Charles Lillyford becomes more than ever anxious that the Two Marriages shall take place.

THE medicines were sent for, and given to Beatrice by her father, who seemed to be the only person that had time to think about her. He led, or rather half carried, her himself up into her own room, and laid her on the bed, thinking she would be more undisturbed there; for though quite unaccustomed to illness, it seemed to him that if it was requisite for her to sleep, she ought to be lying on the bed.

The newly-acquired tenderness caused by anxiety, mingled, perhaps, with a little self-reproach, made him thoughtful. He rang the bell, and told the housemaid who answered it—for Lady Lillyford's maid was occupied in the wedding preparations—to be careful that Miss Lillyford was not disturbed in any way, and to give her the prescribed portion of the medicines.

"In four hours—that will be at seven o'clock," he said, looking at his watch, which, however, as was often the case, he had forgotten to wind. "Well, remember, now, it's three o'clock."

"Yes, Sir Charles, to be sure I will," answered the housemaid. "But, law, sir, Miss Lillyford ain't so ill as all that, is she?"

"Take care, now, shut the door gently," said Sir Charles, who felt more alarmed than he liked to express.

"Well—deary me—and how's the wedding ever to take place on Saturday, and she ill in bed," said the housemaid, as he went downstairs."

But her words, overheard by Sir Charles, awoke a new care in his mind.

"How *can* the wedding take place,"
thought he; "and yet if Sir Bevan comes to
have any idea that her illness proceeds from
disinclination to himself, ten to one he will
suspect that it won't take place at all. Roland's debts will not be paid, and *his* marriage
with Clemmy won't take place. And then
there's that claim hanging over our heads.
Of course the fellow has no right to make it,
but there it is, and who knows how the law
may twist it? And in that case—I mean
supposing it should all go wrong—what
would Roland do without Clemmy's fortune
to fall back upon. Was ever father placed
in such an awkward predicament? Not one.
Why, we should be worse off than ever we
were in our lives—the estate gone, and without the £1,000 a year that my poor cousin
allowed me as his heir—Why, we should
only have the interest of my own £8,000
and Eliza's three—that makes £11,000 in the
Funds, and Roland owes half that. Why,
Beatrice would have no chance at all that

way. No, we must make these marriages go on all right. I—I have a—a—great faith in four and twenty hours' rest—four and twenty hours' rest. That's the thing for her, depend upon it."

His lawyer's opinion had been so far unfavourable, that he recommended, if possible, a compromise, an amicable arrangement of the affair. But if this were attempted before the marriage of his son and daughter, he felt that neither could take place; because he was certain that Clemmy's love for his son was not sufficiently strong to stand the test of a doubtful succession. She evidently looked forward to be mistress of Oakhampton some day. She had let this out in many ways, and his greatest anxiety had been that this dreadful rumour should not reach her ears. Fortunately she had been so taken up with her trousseau, that it seemed for the moment to absorb all her thoughts.

But now, what could be done when Sir

Bevan should call that afternoon, and hear Beatrice was ill in bed?

"Well," he thought, "perhaps it's lucky these women don't believe she's so ill, and they will make the best of it to him. I was wise not to alarm them, if she can but be properly attended to. I must see to this, and I will wait at home to see Sir Bevan myself, too, and see how he takes it."

But to the surprise of the whole household, Sir Bevan never called at all that day, and Sir Charles waited at home until near dinner-time. Then thinking that something untoward must have happened to his future son-in-law, he determined to call at his house and inquire.

Sir Charles had been so harassed all day by all these so strangely complicated distresses, that for the first time in his life he did not care for his dinner, and giving up that hour of supreme happiness—for such it is to a gourmand like Sir Charles—he proceeded direct to Sir Bevan's house.

"Not at home," was the answer, given by the servant who opened the door. "Sir Bevan has not been in since twelve o'clock this morning. Don't know where he's gone—has left no message—went out on foot."

"Had he seen anyone before he went out?—any person on business?" asked Sir Charles.

"Not that we know of; a note was left for him, but the man who brought it did not wait for any answer, and a few minutes afterwards Sir Bevan went out in a great hurry."

"Which way did he go?" inquired Sir Charles of the three or four servants who stood wondering in the hall. "Who saw him go out? Does anyone remember which way?"

"Don't know at all, Sir Charles—think it was up Halkin Street."

"What club does he usually dine at when he does not dine at home?"

The servants did not know, and Sir Charles, therefore, leaving Belgrave Square, called at two or three of which Sir Bevan was a member, but without either finding him, or gaining any intelligence of him.

The disappointed father returned homewards in a state of increased anxiety, and found his wife very cross at having been obliged to put off dinner so long. Yet she was free from the anxiety about her daughter's health, and any of the other evils which were hanging over her head.

" It's lucky she can fret about waiting for her dinner," thought Sir Charles, " and it's only of late that I have learnt to feel there are worse misfortunes than a bad dinner, or —none at all."

CHAPTER XXIX.

Will Marker's Double Game is Unsuccessful.

IN order to account for Sir Bevan Desborough's unwonted absence that day, we must go back to Miss Button's work-room the morning before. It was scarcely one o'clock, and Miss Button had not long returned from her visit to Mary Marker, when she was told that a person had come with a message for her, and was waiting downstairs in the hall to see her. To her surprise, she found it was Will Marker returned already.

"I've found her all safe, and looking very happy," he said, "so now I hope you'll be pleased with me."

"What, at Langton Hall?—yes, it's near

the station; you have been quick—do tell me all, and how you found her out."

"Really can't now—I am in a hurry. I promised to meet somebody who is going to get me something to do. But you need not fear—she's all right. I saw her walking in a pretty garden with a little girl; the child was looking up in her face, as pleased as Punch."

"Well, then, go on."

"I can't tell you any more now, for I have got an engagement; but I will call again by-and-by—say at seven o'clock."

"Oh! I daresay there is nothing more to tell."

"Yes, there is; and besides, with all this business, I haven't had a chance to say—"

"There now, get along," said Miss Button, changing colour slightly, as she shut the door.

"I *must* get along, for it's late," thought he, mechanically feeling for the watch that had long been an *habitué* of the pawnbroker's. He took all the nearest cuts on the way to Belgrave Square, left a note at Sir Bevan's house, which he begged might be given to him immediately, and without waiting for an answer, strolled leisurely through Halkin Street, turned into Lowndes Square, thence through William Street, and crossed over into the Park. Taking the direction of the Magazine, he sauntered on, looking back from time to time, till Sir Bevan joined him under the trees, just about the spot where a motley group used to assemble (I don't know whether they do so still) for the purpose of betting.

Sir Bevan asked him several questions, and then he appeared to meditate profoundly.

Will had thought himself in great luck that day, for by an extraordinary chance the business Sir Bevan employed him about was really the same as that which Lizzy Button had entrusted to him, and therefore he should get paid twice over. Both were anxious to know the whereabouts of the same person. Of course Will Marker kept his own counsel, and did not let the Baronet know that he had already a clue to her discovery, for he wisely imagined such a course would lessen his pay and credit for sharpness with Sir Bevan, who had only been able to discover that the girl of whom he was in search had been employed by Madame Rosalie, and was now missing.

Will fully expected to be further employed by Sir Bevan that day. But in this he was disappointed. Sir Bevan took out his purse, paid him more than the stipulated sum for having done the job so quickly and well; then said, looking at his watch,

"You went there by the ten o'clock train. Well, that will do—stay, come to my house to-morrow morning. There, now you can go."

"He is going to do something about her and won't trust to me," thought Will; "well, he had better have done so, for I'll be even

with him, that I will. He means mischief
to that poor girl—I'm sure he does, by his
face ; and Lizzy is anxious about her, I do
think. I daresay he will go off there by
himself, so I'll just go too by the same train,
and see what's going on. And if I do discover something agin him, why, I'll make
him pay well for keeping his secret—that is,
if it will not be going counter to Lizzy. I'll
circumvent him, at all events."

Will Marker pocketed the money, and set
off in the direction of the City. He went
home first and gave Mary some of his money
to take charge of, desiring her to go and get
a "blow out" (for the breakfast of both had
been rather scanty) ; and Mary, believing it
was Lizzy Button's present, had no scruples
as to how he had come by the money.
Finding, as he proceeded towards the station, that he had plenty of time to spare,
he treated a couple of roystering friends
whom he met on the way, and spent so much
time on the operation, that when he arrived

at the terminus he found that he was too late. The four o'clock train, by which he had intended to travel, was just gone, and there was no other until six that would stop at Langton Bridge. He concluded that Sir Bevan would be obliged to go by the four o'clock train, because no other stopped at this small station, except the early one which had taken Will Marker there in the morning.

He dawdled about the station until six o'clock, then took his place in a second-class-carriage, and was set down at Langton Bridge station about a quarter before seven. He saw a crowd on the platform, and heard one of the porters say to a servant in livery, "What, is the young lady not yet found?"

"No—nothing heard of her," was the reply; "my master and Mr. Stanway be in a pretty way up at Langton Hall, I believe you."

The name caught Will's quick ears, and he

edged himself in with the crowd to hear the rest of the dialogue.

"Which way do you think she went?" inquired the porter.

"Nobody knows; excepting that she was decoyed away out of the garden by somebody as beckoned to her when Mr. Stanway's grandchild was walking with her."

"What sort of a looking young lady was she?"

"Well, she only came to our place the night before last, so I have not justly looked at her; but she is small, and white in the face; with great dark eyes that look you through and through; and she is deaf and dumb."

"When was she missed?"

"She went out in the garden with the children after luncheon, and she has not been seen or heard of since four o'clock. Me, the coachman and Mr. Stanway, has been looking for her all over the country,—we came here to the station first, two hours ago, but the station-master don't know nothing, nor the guard of the train as came in, and——"

"Any tidings, John?" said a tall, dark gentleman who strode up at that moment, looking extremely agitated, and addressed the footman.

"None at all, sir," said the latter, touching his hat. "I was just asking the porter about it; but he hasn't seen no young lady to-day hereabouts but what could speak for herself."

A younger-looking man, who also appeared very anxious and unhappy, now came up to the group, and the tall one who had just spoken said a few words to him, which Will Marker could not hear; but the reply was,

"Well, then, Sterndale, you see she cannot have gone up by the train, or these people would know. Let us go to your aunt, Mrs. Stanway, and tell her that we are going to pursue our search in some of the villages round,—or stay, let us first inquire at the inn, whoever took her away may have had horses from there."

Will Marker thus ascertained that the taller of the two speakers was Mr. Sterndale, and that he was nephew to the lady (Mrs. Stanway) with whom the poor girl had been staying.

"This is Sir Bevan's doing, I'll be bound," thought Will. "What a fool I was not to have followed him, and seen which way he went. She was missed at four o'clock—then he must have come down from London by road as hard as four posters could lay leg to ground, or he must have come by express to Barford, and then here by road. What an idiot I was to let him give me the slip! But it's too late now to grumble. I must do the best I can to circumvent him; for Lizzy would never forgive me if she found that I had helped Sir Bevan to do the girl a bad turn, and she is one of them as finds out everything."

Making inquiries of some other people who were standing about the station, Will Marker gathered further that Mrs. Stanway's little grandchild could give no other reason for the deaf and dumb girl's disappearance, than that a big, dark man with a red face had beckoned to her from the other side of the gate; but the child did not understand what was said. She seemed to have waited some time for the Italian girl (who had gone out of sight with the strange gentleman), and called repeatedly, until getting tired at last of running about there, she returned home. But it must have been nearly an hour afterwards before she was missed, as the child thought she would come back when she liked, and said nothing about her absence.

Finding that Mr. Sterndale and his friend could not obtain any satisfactory information at the station, Will Marker determined to go and explore on the road to Stonycross, for he had reasons of his own for thinking it possible she might have been taken away in that direction; and as some conveyance must have been had for the purpose, he decided to inquire. He walked about a quarter of a mile, and when he had reached a small detached cottage standing back in a field at a little distance, where some children were playing in the garden, he stopped and asked them whether they had seen a carriage pass that way.

"Yes," said a little boy; "and the horses—they were four—went so fast we could not catch it up, though we tried so very hard."

"Which way?" said Will.

The child pointed on the road to Stony-cross.

"But which way did you first see it come—for it must have come from somewhere before it went away."

"No, I never see it before."

"Yes, but *I* did," said a little girl. "I saw it come along down that there hill when I was over there in the Picket-piece. It waited in that hollow down there, for I wondered what it came into there for, which that lane don't go nowheres."

" You saw it waiting? Can you remember how long?"

" Oh! a good bit, 'cause I picked ever so many cowslips."

" And did you see anybody get into the carriage?"

" No, 'cause we could only see the top on him."

" How long has it been gone away?"

The poor children had not much idea of time—they only scratched their heads and looked stupid. Will, who knew how precious that article, as he called it, was, on such an occasion as this, hastened back to the town to see whether he could get a conveyance. As he ran on quickly, he meditated whether he should inform Mr. Sterndale of his suspicions, and then obtain more help to extricate the girl in case of need.

" But my face is against me," thought he ;

" they'll think I'm a sharper, or some one in league with the man who took her away. Well, I can but try, for I should for once like to do a good turn, even if I don't get paid for it; and somehow that girl's face keeps coming up before me, and I should not like to think she was ill-treated."

CHAPTER XXX.

What has become of Fronica?

WHEN Will Marker arrived at Langton Bridge, he saw Mr. Sterndale and the other gentleman just stepping into a dog-cart, so there was no time to be lost.

" Please sir," he said, touching his hat, trying to look as respectable as he could, and addressing the younger and more kindly looking of the two—"please, sir, I think if you be going to look after that poor young lady that has disappeared, I might be able to help you to find her."

" *You?*" exclaimed the taller and sterner of the two. " Why? Do you know her?"

" No, but an acquaintance of mine is—is very anxious about her; and I should like to help find her, if possible."

"And who is your acquaintance who cares for the poor girl?"

"Please, sir, it's Miss Button, who lives with the great milliner, Madame Rosalie, and the deaf and dumb girl was there too."

"Ah! I see. Well, and how do you know where she is gone?"

"I don't *know*, but I think it's just possible I might find her, because—well, I'd rather not say if I could help it, because it might get me into trouble—for the party who I think may have done this has been—has helped me when I was in distress."

"Do you mean Sir Bevan Desborough?"

"Well, I'd rather not say—but we're losing time—and time is everything in this case."

"How far, and where do you think she may be?"

"About twelve miles off, at Stonycross; perhaps I could get a horse and follow, for I'd make the cart too heavy."

"Yes," said Mr. Sterndale, who called to

the landlord of the inn. A horse was soon found, and they started on the Stonycross road.

"Strange, is it not? A wild-looking fellow that, but clever," said Mr. Sterndale to his companion. " I think he would make a good detective—but I doubt his honesty. Come, cheer up, Arthur. Now I hope we shall be in time to stop this hateful marriage. God grant it may be so; but his having hastened it shows he must be well prepared. What a fool I was not to caution Henry more—and not to say that my aunt must not lose sight of the girl! Still, I never imagined he could track her here. He must have spies about everywhere."

"You never told me the origin of your suspicion that Fronica is Sir Bevan's daughter—I mean when you first began to investigate this affair?"

"My dear fellow, I never had time—it's only since I heard that poor girl Beatrice was going to be sacrificed, that I saw the necessity for accurate inquiry. Before that, I was so full of this other business of Edward Luscombe's, that I was directing all my energies to it. Well, if we can only find her I'll tell you the story from the very beginning. I want just to say a word now to that odd and suspicious-looking vagabond."

"I think he has a heart, though," said Arthur.

"Ho! what's your name?"

"Will Marker, sir."

"Where did you live before—before you took to a wild London life?"

"At Westfield, about a mile from Langton Bridge on this road—and that's how I come to know all about these here parts so well; it's where my sister and I was born and bred; and Lizzy Button also come from hereabouts, and she got herself put a prentice to a milliner in London, and then Mary and I thought we'd go and try our luck there too."

"But as to this Miss Button of yours. I

want to know why you think she is really
interested about this poor deaf and dumb
girl."

"'Cause she told me—and she were sorry.
I saw the tears come into her eyes when she
was afraid she was lost : and she gave me a
good bit of money to pay my expenses in
looking for her—and—and that is how I
came to know she was at Langton."

"And how came you down here now?—
are you living here?"

"No, sir, I live with my sister, sir, in London. She is very good indeed, sir, and works
hard, she does—never rests from morning to
night. I wish, sir, you'd go and see my sister—for you would believe me then. I
know I'm a good-for-nothing chap, and had
not a ought to it, when I've had such a good
sister—a good sister as Mary is to me ; and
I half broke her heart after——"

"Where do you say she lives ?"

"No. 16, Blank Court, Crutched Friars."

Mr. Sterndale made a note of it ; and

then said, " What have you done with your earnings?—lost them at betting, I suppose, or gambling."

" That's pretty near the truth—but I ain't going for to go on so—much longer. I should so much like to set up in business—and—and get a wife—I should indeed, sir."

" Well, I daresay your happiness is in your own power—if you will but persevere."

" Ah, sir—that's just it."

" Well—what now do you suppose Sir Bevan has done with the girl ?"

" Can't say—but there's a old servant of his, an old nurse, lives at Stonycross—and it's my belief she's one as wouldn't stand at nothing if she was well paid for it."

" But I doubt whether he would leave her there," said Mr. Sterndale, after a moment's thought. " I'm afraid he will try to get her across the channel."

" Well, they must get fresh horses first, I should say, if they dont get on the rail— where it's easier to be pursued on—because they can't turn and twist, as hosses can, without a-shewing of theirselves to get tickets and sich like."

"Very true," said Mr. Sterndale. "We'll hope, at all events, to discover some clue from this person at Stonycross;" and urging on the horse, they proceeded at greater speed—Will following as fast as his horse, which was not quite in such good condition, was able to do.

"I think that man is not deceiving us," said Mr. Sterndale—"it seems evident to me that whatever good feelings he has by nature are now in the ascendant; and I believe in that sister of his, for his roguish eyes had a different look when he spoke of her. I believe that she is a better woman than his Lizzy Button; for I take it that is the very girl who snatched that note out of poor Fronica's hand."

"Well—but with regard to this deaf and dumb girl—how did you come to know so much about her?"

Mr. Sterndale was silent for a moment, and then said,

"Ah, it's a strange story that—it sounds like a bit out of the Mysteries of Udolpho. But truth *is* stranger than fiction. There is no truer proverb than that. I was just thinking of telling you about it; but the story is so long, that I am afraid of not being able to finish it before we get to the place this man is taking us to."

"Never mind about breaking it off—you can finish it afterwards," said Arthur.

CHAPTER XXXI.

Fronica's early History.

"WELL, then," said Mr. Sterndale, giving a nervous flip in the air with his whip, and drawing himself up on the driving-seat. "This is the story—and a very queer one it is to be mixed up with—even if I had not—I mean if there were no further interest in it than one had in an exciting novel or a play. Thirteen years ago, I happened to take notice of a child gathering flowers under the heights of Posilipo—quite by herself.

"I was struck by the earnest, almost appealing expression of her eyes; and I stood still at a little distance to look at her. She seemed tired, and as there were no houses near, it occurred to me that she might have strayed away from home, and got too far; perhaps farther than she knew. So I went up to speak to her—intending to give her a lift in the carriage, which was waiting for me near (I was going on a longish expedition), and set her down at her home. I found that the expressive eyes which I noticed was her only utterance,—she was deaf and dumb.

"By means of signs, and her own intelligence, which was unusually great for her age, I was able to discover that I had been correct in supposing she had strayed too far, and couldn't find her way home. This was a very awkward difficulty for me, but I was extraordinarily interested in her; and besides, how could I leave a child of six or seven years old, who had lost her way? I made signs to her that I would take her home; and the little trustful thing followed me at once without any hesitation.

"Just as we reached the carriage which

was waiting for me about a hundred yards off, a peasant passed, and I asked her if she knew where the child lived. To my great relief she said that she did, and pointed in the direction of the house—telling me, at the same time, the name of the people who lived there. Well, I drove to the house, and knocked at the door; a youngish woman answered it. Pointing to the child, I told her in a few words why I had come there. I found that she was the child's aunt; and an old woman, who proved to be the grandmother, came to the door, on hearing my voice.

"They seemed very cross with the child for having strayed away—but did not thank me for bringing her; which surprised me, for the Neapolitans are usually good-humoured, and fond of children. I asked the aunt whose child it was, but she pretended not to understand me, and said something in the Neapolitan dialect which I could not make out. So there was nothing left but to go away;

but somehow I was so anxious to know more, that I set my clever *valet de place* to find out what he could about them.

"A few days afterwards he told me that the aunt was a maker of artificial flowers, and that the child was in the habit of picking bouquets for her to copy. She made them for a convent near, where the nuns sold them for her. I would not go to the hut again until my valet had made further investigations, for they had evidently not seemed much pleased at my notice of the child. He had difficulty in obtaining any other information, but at last he heard that some of their relations were 'cattiva gente,' and one or two of the neighbours told him that the little girl was the daughter of an English milord, and that her mother was dead. I asked a friend to take me to the convent where the aunt took her flowers, and, under pretence of buying some, inquired whether they knew a little deaf and dumb girl named Fronica. I had found out that was her name.

"'Ah, si!' said a kind-looking old sister, 'and we want her to be taken to the school for the deaf and dumb. But her old grandmother cannot be prevailed on to part with her, though we have offered to pay her expenses. It is a sad history, for the child's mother was a beautiful girl, and very good, too. But unfortunately an English lady took a great fancy to her, and persuaded her to go to England with her. She only went with her as far as Rome, when a milord married her.

"'Si, davvero,' she added, on seeing I suppose an incredulous look on my face. 'Lo so benissimo, for the poor girl told me herself, when she returned, that Padre Antonio performed the marriage ceremony at Rome.'

"I asked her who was the milord.

"'Ah, per questo non lo so,' she replied, shaking her head, 'for the English names are so difficult to pronounce. But I do know it began with a D.   Our good confessor was quite satisfied that she was married, although she returned home without a soldo —only to give birth to this poor little child. She was quite broken-hearted at the desertion of her husband, and all thonght she must die.   But she lived for two years, I think, and then she disappeared.   No one was in the house when she went away, but the mother and sister took it into their heads that it was the wicked husband who carried her off.   This is why they do not like the English at all, and the old woman is always afraid the child will be taken from her.' All this the old sister told me.

"As I was going from Naples to Sicily in a few days, I went once more to the cottage and endeavoured again to mollify her relations.   But I found it very difficult; perhaps all the more so because the child herself seemed to have taken a liking for me. When I returned to Naples the following spring I found that the old nun's arguments had prevailed; the child had gone to the asylum, and they said she had proved remarkably intelligent. I procured Padre Antonio's direction, but subsequently found that he had gone on some distant mission. Thus I was baffled for the time being in my endeavour to find out the name of Fronica's father; however, I still resolved to persevere in my investigations, whenever I had an opportunity.

" But I must get on with my story; for we can't be very far from the place. Six years afterwards I was in Italy again, and I saw her at the asylum. I found her developing into a beautiful and clever creature. I tried again, by various means, to find out who she was—but could make nothing of it, and that same winter was recalled to England by my father's illness. Then you know for upwards of a year after his death I was engaged in settling his affairs, and arranging those of my mother and sister. In short, I was not able to go abroad again until the winter of 18——, and then I went direct to Naples, for the express purpose of seeing how she was going on.

"There all was changed: the grandmother dead—the aunt a cripple, and in such distress, that she had consented to send Fronica to a shop in Florence, to make flowers. I went to this shop. I found she was no longer there; an English lady, struck by her beauty, had taken her as companion, and had offered a large salary.

"However, I did not despair of hearing about her, for an advertisement in the *Times* I thought would be sure to find her out, so I went to make a long intended tour in Calabria.

"It was fortunate that I did so. You know my love for exploring wild scenes, and seeing nature under all its different aspects. I put an old silver watch into my pocket instead of my own, slung a knapsack on my back, and leaving my servant and luggage at a little inn of one of the villages, I set out one morning for a few days' ramble among the mountains. I met with many curious incidents and strange sights, which I will tell you another time; but now to shorten this long history.

"After I had rambled about a few days, I came upon a zig-zag path, leading up to a curious old castle or tower, very picturesquely situated. I sat down and took out my pocket-book, to make a sketch of the scene, when I was startled by hearing the notes of a very beautiful and plaintive melody, as of some one singing. I gazed round, and presently thought it seemed to come from the summit of the tower; and looking up I saw the form of a woman at one of the high windows. Her face was very pale—the southern olive complexion—masses of black hair fell over, and partly concealed her neck and shoulders. When she saw me the song ceased; but she gazed down upon me with melancholy eyes, which affected me strongly, and reminded me of some one I had seen, or some dream I must have dreamed. I felt an irresistible impulse to speak to her—to ask her who she was.

"I hastened up the path, and arrived at the base of the tower—the entrance, a massive archway, was on a different side from where I had seen the figure, and did not command the lovely view down the valley which had excited my sketching propensities. All seemed deserted. I knocked, and tried to make as much noise as I could, when an old hag emerged stealthily from a side door and asked what I wanted.

" 'I am an artist,' I said, showing my sketch ; 'let me see the view from the top of the tower.'

" ' No, no, no,' she said, ' no one goes up there !   Hush !"

" I took a coin out of my pocket, and held it up before her.

" ' No, no !' she said.   ' It is as much as my life is worth. Roderigo will be back here at sundown. Roderigo—he would marry my poor Beata, who died of this wild life, and now I have to keep house for him here.'

" 'There are two hours to sundown,' I said. I took a ducat from my pocket, and shewed it to her. ' Five of these,' I said with my fingers—*cinque;* ' if you will let me go up, I will not stay above a minute.'

" The old woman's eyes glistened, and she nodded slowly; then disappeared again, and came out presently with two great keys. With one of these she unlocked the heavy gate, and then we entered a square court-yard. On her way she turned round upon me suddenly, and whispered—

" ' But she is mad.'

" 'Never mind,' I said. ' Remember five pieces—to let me go up. But why do you shut her up here ?'

" 'She is Roderigo's prisoner, and I and Peppina take charge of her—oh ! she is well cared for, she wants for nothing.'

" On the other side of the courtyard we

went through a doorway, up a wide stone staircase. Though half in ruins now, it must formerly have been a stately dwelling. We passed through a suite of rooms, where the remains of good painting on the wall and ceiling were all visible, and where the windows opened on a broad walk which overhung the steep ravine, and, here and there, was built out beyond it. At the end of this suite was a circular turret, with a narrow winding stair in one corner. This we mounted one by one, and at the top the old woman undid the bolts of a strong door. We found ourselves in a more comfortable-looking room than I had expected to find in such a ruined place; and near the oriel window, which commanded a splendid view, sat the poor woman. She was looking out into the far distance with a kind of fixed gaze, which certainly did not take in its beauty, for her countenance was most sad. She did not look round, or take any notice of us.

"'Hist, Madama,' said the old woman, to arrest her attention. 'Ecco un Francese.'

"You remember that in the kingdom of Naples the peasantry are apt to call all foreigners Frenchmen.

"'Inglese,' I said in an accent which, to any dispassionate hearer, must have settled the question.

"'Inglese,' said she, starting round, and looking at me full in the face, with an expression of countenance that made me think I had put my foot in it, somehow or other. Suddenly it flashed across my mind who it was she had reminded me of. It was Fronica.

"'Dammi mia figlia! Give me my child!' she said piteously, clasping her hands. 'I only want her. Let me see her once more, poverina, and then I will die content.'

"I asked her where her child was.

"'In Napoli, povera, e sorda e muta. She was born deaf and dumb, because my heart was broken by——'

"' E quasi pazza !' said the old woman.

" 'Is your child Fronica ?' I inquired.

"' Si, si; Fronica, dammi mia figlia, dammi!' and she tried to throw herself on her knees before me.

" I asked her the name of her husband. But at that moment the old woman interrupted me, saying hurriedly,

"' Basta cosi, if you question her any more she will get furious. Come away, now.'

" I could not make out whether the old woman had her own reasons for wishing to keep the secret, and dreaded merely that it might be dangerous to disclose too much, or that her quick eye saw something in the distance that made her wish to get rid of me. Whichever it was, she was so resolute about getting me away, that I saw I should only make a mess of the whole business by attempting to stay, so I left the room, determining to take an accurate observation of the place, so as to make use of what I had seen and heard as soon as I could have a chance of doing so. On my way downstairs, I asked by whose wish the poor woman was shut up in the tower. She affected not to understand. I asked her again, but I found that I could get nothing more out of her; so I paid her the five ducats, and made the best of my way out of the valley. I returned to Naples immediately, and took an immense deal of trouble to ferret out the mystery; and, by comparing a great many circumstances that came to my knowledge, I became morally certain that the husband of the maniac (if she was mad, which I very much doubt) and the father of the deaf and dumb girl, was no other than Sir Bevan Desborough."

"What a thundering scoundrel!" muttered Arthur,

"And," continued Mr. Sterndale, "if anything more was necessary to make me certain that he is the man, I have it now, in the fact of his having carried off Fronica—

thus proving that he had something to dread from her evidence."

"But what did you do about her, the poor, imprisoned wife?"

"Well, I was circumvented about that; I suspect the old woman sold me, after pocketing the five ducats, for inquiries were made, at my request, by the authorities, and it was found· that no people answering my description were then living at the place I had indicated; therefore, don't you see, I can't as yet bring home to him the fact of a living wife. But I have put more irons in the fire about it, and I am expecting every day, as you know, to hear something. I have heard enough to make me have very little doubt of the result; but the time is running short, and my fear is that the letter may arrive too late."

Arthur Fairleigh turned very pale and bit his lips.

"Go on," he said, trying very hard to appear calm.

"That is the reason," continued Mr. Sterndale, "why I am so anxious to nail him to-night, for if I can catch him detaining Fronica against her will, he must either give her up, and therefore leave her free to stop his present game, or else he must acknowledge her to be his daughter, which would come practically to the same thing."

"They won't believe the story," said Arthur, "unless you get the proof of his wife being alive now. If Beatr—Miss Lilly-ford had not been satisfied with him she would——"

"Don't be an ass!" drily remarked his companion. "Don't you know that there are a hundred thousand ways of putting on the screw—a hundred thousand possibilities that would make your judgment about it as unjust as it is unreasonable."

CHAPTER XXXII.

What passed in the Old Gabled House.

"I HOPE that Will Marker is not leading us a wild goose-chase, at all events," said Arthur Fairleigh after a pause, during which Mr. Sterndale and himself had been proceeding at a slackened pace, along what seemed a rough cross road.

"Well, we shall soon know; we must have come nearly the twelve miles by this time, I should think."

A minute afterwards they passed through a long, straggling village; a little beyond which, at a bend of the road, Will Marker called out to them to stop. They did so; and he, motioning for them to follow, turned down a narrow lane to the right, at the end of which, about a quarter of a mile off, was a cottage or farm-house, standing in a garden a good way back from the road. They could just see the outline of its pointed gables against the sky. But no lights were visible in any of the windows.

"Wait here," whispered Will; "and don't speak loud enough to be heard. Please to hold the horse while I go round to the back of the house and see if there are any, lights anywhere. She is a cautious old screw; but if I can get round and look in at the kitchen window, I may be able to find out what they are at. And you had better keep watch here, and see that no one leaves the house by the front door."

The two friends passed the time in silence, while the rain, which now began to fall, drenched them as they stood shelterless on the road, and pattered heavily on the gables of the old house with a monotonous sound, which did not tend to raise their spirits. At one moment Arthur fancied that a light gleamed between the shutters of one of the upper windows, but it disappeared so quickly that Mr. Sterndale, who was rather short-sighted, thought it must have been a fancy of Arthur's.

Nearly a quarter of an hour passed, and as Will Marker had not returned they began to get very impatient, and were beginning to consult together what they had better do, when a rustling in the garden hedge was heard, and Will Marker stealthily appeared.

"Hist! come a little farther from the house, and I will tell you. I do think somebody is there, and yet I could not make anyone hear. The kitchen fire is a-light, and som'at is roasting by it, so I suppose some one is with her, and he be a-going to have supper there. I should advise you gentlemen to watch while I go to the public-house in the village, which is kept by this woman's sister, and maybe I shall find Mrs. Perkins herself there. I'm afraid she's over-fond of strong waters, and might even forget to come back here for ever so long, while the poor lady may be locked up in one of those top rooms with good shutters, and we can't see nothing of what's going on up there."

They were quite willing to remain; but Arthur suggested that perhaps he had better go with Marker, to which Mr. Sterndale agreed.

The two horses and dog-cart were left with Mr. Sterndale in the lane, for they did not wish to attract more attention than could be avoided. Fortunately there was a good deal of grass at the sides of the road, and Mr. Sterndale, who regarded with more regret the supperless and exposed condition of the poor animals than he did his own discomfort, contrived that they should have the full benefit of the green turf.

This done, he set himself to watch the house, thinking she might possibly try to look out of one of the windows. Being deaf, she could of course hear no sound or call that he could make to attract her attention; but he thought, if he could procure a light, it might show her that she had a friend near.

With this view he took out a box of flaming fusees from his pocket, and lighted one, holding it up close to his face that the light might shine on his features, while he looked up anxiously at the upper windows.

He fancied that he heard a sound just afterwards, like a slight tap at a window pane or the movement of a shutter, but it was too dark to distinguish anything except the dark spaces which showed where the windows were.

Presently afterwards he heard a footstep coming across the garden. Nearer and nearer it came; evidently it was the heavy tread of a man's boots. Then a sudden dread seized Mr. Sterndale that he might have betrayed his presence to the very person he was anxious to circumvent—that Sir Bevan Desborough was there, and had recognized him.

Then he heard the garden gate swing on its hinges, and a tall figure could be just discerned against the sky. Fortunately it turned the other way, and Mr. Sterndale heard the footsteps gradually recede, till they were no longer audible; but about a minute afterwards he thought he heard the sound of carriage wheels, and they seemed to be going in the opposite direction also, for the sound soon died away, and all was quiet again. " It must be Sir Bevan, and his carriage was probably waiting for him at a little distance on the other road," thought Mr. Sterndale. " Now, if we could but effect an entrance into the house, Fronica might be rescued."

It was certainly like his tall large figure; and he was alone, for there was just light enough at the open space where the gate was to show if he had been accompanied by anyone. Even *her* slight and fairy-like form," he thought, " must have been visible had she been there." He felt now more convinced that this man was really Sir Bevan, and that consequently Fronica must be in that house. Yet how could he leave that poor girl—his own daughter—alone and unprotected in such a desolate place? Had he really no heart? And, in spite of his anxiety, Mr. Sterndale began to speculate as to what kind and degree of happiness a man like Sir Bevan can be capable of feeling, who sacrifices everything to gain the indulgence of a present fancy.

CHAPTER XXXIII.

A Telegram is sent to Mrs. Dronington.

WHEN Dr. Pillcox called that evening in Portman Square he found that Beatrice had not been able to sleep, and was in the same excited state as before. In reply to his question as to what she suffered from, she complained of her head, but was unable to describe what it was that she felt. In answer to his further inquiries, she added that she had great difficulty in thinking, and was much tormented by visions of faces and figures.

Clemmy, who had become somewhat alarmed about her towards evening, was sitting in the room when the doctor came, and Dr. Pillcox asked her as he was going away whether she had been talking at all to Miss Lillyford.

"Very little," answered Clemmy. "She wanted to ask me a few questions, but I tried not to encourage her talking."

"Quite right; she must be kept as quiet as possible, and repeat the sedative. I will write another prescription downstairs, which must be sent for immediately."

"Now, darling," said Clemmy, as soon as he was gone down; "you must not say another word—do try to be happy, and go to sleep."

"Only just one word," said Beatrice, "before my mind quite goes, for I really feel so odd. I suppose I must be dying. Do see your mother, do, I can't bear the idea of her not being at your wedding; promise me she shall be there."

"Well, I will, if it will make you happier, darling."

"There's another thing," said Beatrice; "will you tell grandmamma how ill I am,

and how I want to see her ; ask papa again before—before—oh ! my poor head, I can't
think. Do ask him to come up here directly."

Miss Gubbings went downstairs, and found
Sir Charles with Dr. Pillcox, both looking
very grave, and the former very anxious.

" She wants to see you," said Clemmy to
Sir Charles, "before she goes to sleep, for
she has promised to try and be happy."

" I'll come at once; but there is no—
there cannot be any immediate danger ?" he
said, turning to Dr. Pillcox.

" Unless she can sleep, I fear that brain-
fever must ensue. If there is anything on
her mind, you must endeavour to remove it,
if you can. It seems to me as if she was
living in the constant apprehension of something she dreads, and this has unhinged her
body and mind completely. Good night."

All this was said in the same kind of ab-
rupt, hard tone, and with a business-like
manner that seemed to take all feeling out
of it, and to leave an impression of doubt on

any listener whose heart was in the matter, whether the case was really bad or not.

Sir Charles was puzzled, for he had begun to feel anxious about Beatrice; but he repeated the doctor's words over to himself again, and then forgetting Dr. Pillcox's cold manner, became impressed by a sense of danger, and ran upstairs to her room, followed by Clemmy, who for the moment became rather frightened, or rather she felt slightly provoked with Lady Lillyford for persisting in saying that there was nothing the matter.

And yet this delusion or indifference of the mother was in favour of Clemmy's own plans; for the illness must be made the best of—because if Sir Bevan should think that the wedding could not take place on the Saturday, he would refuse to liberate Roland the evening before. So she determined that Sir Charles should pacify Beatrice, by promising that everything should be as she wished.

They found that the poor girl's greatest anxiety was to see her grandmother once more. If her father would but send for her she promised to abide by Mrs. Dronington's advice; but she "could not—oh! it was impossible," she said, "she must die if she were forced to marry without her grandmother's advice."

"There, I see that face again!" she cried out. "Oh! papa, pray, pray do not let him come near me! Oh! save me from him, and I will try—I will——"

"What face, darling?—there is no one but me."

(Clemmy had remained in the shadow of the doorway.)

"There, it comes between us!"

He came close and kissed her fevered brow, and said,

"I will send at once for your grandmamma—I will telegraph for her. There, will that satisfy you?"

"Oh! thank you, dear papa. When—when will she be able to come?"

"Oh! I daresay by to-morrow evening; and now you will try to sleep, will you?"

"Yes, if—if you really will send."

"Indeed I will, darling; I will go this very moment and write a line, and send John to the telegraph office at once. There, now, I see you will be happy, darling, and go to sleep."

Sir Charles had not intended to send for Mrs. Dronington, because he feared her presence would sadly interfere with all their plans; but when he became alarmed by the wild look and incoherent words of Beatrice, he began to fear that if her grandmother did not arrive before the wedding, she would really be too ill, and that the ceremony must be postponed. So he only hoped to be able to make the old lady see reason, and by informing her of the urgency of the case, and the dangers that threatened them, he might enlist her sympathy on what he still considered to be the right side.

Some such vague ideas crossed his mind as he went downstairs to write the telegram. But Clemmy did not approve of this, and determined it should not go, for she had a far deeper insight into Mrs. Dronington's character than Sir Charles, and was convinced that no help could be obtained from that "prim old thing," as she called her. But it was better Sir Charles should think that she was coming, so she went down with him to the library, and stood by as he wrote the message.

"Yes," she said, looking over the paper, "that will do very well; but you had better go and sit with Beatrice a little, till she goes to sleep, and I will ring and give this to John. I strongly advise you not to tell Lady Lillyford that you have sent for her mother, for it will put her out sadly; and as she persists in thinking Beatrice is not really ill, it will only bother and frighten her for nothing; and, you know, we shall be able to manage Sir Bevan much better if Lady Lillyford does not think Beatrice is ill, for he will easily see that she is not alarmed, and that, you know, is a great comfort, and will be very useful to us. Now go back at once to Beatrice, and I will do this up and direct it."

CHAPTER XXXIV.

Sir Charles Lillyford sees the force of Clemmy's Reasonings, and they are both anxious about Sir Bevan Desborough.

SIR CHARLES fully saw the force of her reasoning, and resolved to say nothing to Lady Lillyford, as it would be time enough when Mrs. Dronington arrived to explain how it was.

But all this time they had heard nothing of Sir Bevan Desborough. Clemmy felt as uneasy and as much perplexed as Sir Charles at his non-appearance. So he determined that, after sitting a little while with Beatrice, he would go out again, and see whether he might have returned home.

"I have sent the telegram for your grandmother," said he, as he sat down by her bedside, for he saw that she was not asleep, and was looking fixedly at something straight before her. "I have indeed," he repeated; "so now—won't you shut your eyes, darling?—pray do," he said, as he kissed her again, and felt how burning hot her cheeks were.

"I will try, dear papa, and thank you for being so kind to me."

She then shut her eyes, and after waiting by her side for a few minutes, he had the satisfaction of thinking that she had really sunk into a quiet sleep. So he walked softly across the room, and having placed the light so that it might not shine on her face, he opened the door and found Clemmy outside. They both proceeded with noiseless steps downstairs.

"She is going to sleep, is she not?" Clemmy inquired, when they had reached the drawing-room landing.

"I hope so; and I think now I will go

and see if there are any tidings of Sir Bevan."

" Ah! do," said Clemmy; " I am very much alarmed about him."

" Why?—have you any particular reason besides the strangeness of his not coming here to-day?"

" Not exactly; but——"

" Well, I am determined to ascertain, if possible, where he is before I go to bed to-night."

" Yes, do, and I will sit up till you come back; but I will make Lady Lillyford go to bed, for she will be more cross and out of sorts to-morrow if she gets tired and anxious. It is most fortunate that she does not think Beatrice really ill; so pray do not try to alarm her."

" No—but pray take care that she does not disturb the poor girl, for you know everything depends upon her being able to sleep. Ha! what is that?—a carriage at the door?—perhaps it is Sir Bevan," and they both looked over the balustrades in great anxiety.

But they soon ascertained it was only their own carriage, which had been ordered in the morning, and before they had become alarmed about Beatrice, to take them to a party at Mrs. Winchfield's, and no one had thought of countermanding it. Lady Lillyford had said at dinner-time that she supposed no one would go, but that she was not sorry, for she was really so worn out that she had scarcely energy to dress. "Though I had intended to wear my new white and cerise dress," she said; "dear Mrs. Winchfield does notice and admire my dress so much."

Clemmy remembered now that Lady Lillyford said this at dinner, although at the time she had been too anxious about many more important matters to heed or answer her observations.

"Well," she said, "how lucky it's come,

for now you can drive down to Belgrave Square in it."

"So it is," said Sir Charles; " I will take it—but I shan't want my servant. I suppose John has not returned from the telegraph-office?"

No, John had not returned, nor did he for some time, because Clemmy had given him some other commissions to do; and he was also delayed a little at the office, because the message had been difficult to decipher.

CHAPTER XXXV.

Mrs. Dronington hears some news of Rachel Harraway.

AT the very same hour that Sir Charles was driving off to search for his missing son-in-law, Mrs. Dronington, at the distance of a hundred and fifty miles, was anxiously watching by the sick-bed of her favourite niece. She had been surprised not to hear from Beatrice for some time, and had written several letters to her, having heard rumours of her intended marriage; which letters, as we before mentioned, Beatrice had never received. Mrs. Dronington had made several inquiries in her letters about Sir Bevan.

In her last letter Lady Lillyford had said

that he was very handsome and gentleman-
like, and that he had acted so generously
with regard to Roland and his debts, that
she trusted and hoped Beatrice would show
her gratitude for his kindness to her brother,
by not opposing the match, as it would in
every way be most advantageous for her darling child. But when she wrote the letter no
day had been positively fixed, so that she
did not think it necessary to say more. This
letter was written by Lady Lillyford, but
dictated by Clemmy, who thought it better
to give the old lady some idea of what was
going on, lest she should hear the truth
through some other channel, and becoming
alarmed about her grandchild, might arrive
in London at an awkward moment.

It so happened that Mrs. Dronington had
not heard any reports about Sir Bevan that
caused her to dread that he was not calcu-
lated to make her grandchild happy, for she
had lived out of the world so long that gossip connected with the present day seldom

reached her ear.   But on this very evening, when the telegram ought to have reached her, she was destined to hear several facts about Sir Bevan from a most unexpected source.   The nurse who had attended her niece had become quite worn out with her long attendance, and was obliged to go home and lay herself up for a time.   She recommended another, an old friend of her own, who lived in the next parish ; she had given up regular practice as a nurse, but to oblige a friend she might be induced to come.

"Whom has she attended?" inquired Mrs. Dronington, who did not at all like the idea of having a stranger about her poor niece.

"She lived for several years with the late Lady Desborough," said the nurse ; "and she were so fond of Mrs. Gwin that she left her enough to live on, so that she never need go out any more."

"With the late Lady Desborough—indeed ! and when did the poor lady die ?"

"Better nor a year ago, I think ; and I'll

make bold to say you'll like Mrs. Gwin so much that you'll be very sorry, you will, to get me back again. Several ladies has told me as much."

"Well, then, if you feel you are sure we shall like the nurse, send her as soon as you can."

In less than an hour after, Mrs. Gwin came. She was old, and looked worn, yet her eyes had a restless and unsettled look that Mrs. Dronington did not quite like; so she determined to talk to her a little before she installed her by her niece's bedside. She began by inquiring how long she had lived with Lady Desborough?

"Going on for six years, ma'am; for her ladyship was never very well from the time she married Sir Bevan."

"Oh! an habitual invalid, was she?"

"Not entirely, for at times she got a little better; but the poor lady had too many troubles."

"Was Sir Bevan kind to her?"

Mrs. Gwin looked up as if she was surprised, and seemed to think before she answered the question, then said,

"I suppose you was not acquainted with Sir Bevan, mum?"

"I never saw him, nor have I heard much about him."

"Well, mum, least said is soonest mended, and it's not for me to start that hare, nor to say more than is needful, and—it's no business of mine, neither," added Mrs. Gwin, as if she was forcibly checking herself from speaking.

"Does Sir Bevan give you this allowance, or pension, for having taken such good care of his wife?"

"He do—leastways, they say my lady mentioned me in her will; but that's neither here nor there, for I don't know nothing about lawyers, and such like business, but I does get £40 a year, paid regular, and that's enough for me."

"I'm afraid he was not very kind to his

wife," said Mrs. Dronington, who was puzzled with the woman's manner and words.

"Well, mum, I can't say as he was, and yet he never let her out of his sight, which he allays took her with him, he did, in all the foreign parts, though it did tire the poor lady, sure enough; but he pretended—that is, he said, he could never bear to leave her alone; but," she added, checking herself, " which, as I said before, it's not for me to start that hare."

"Sir Bevan is very rich, isn't he?"

"My lady was. It was all her fortune; and she didn't care for nothing, surely, except some one to care about her. Poor lady! she did pine for that; and her friends they was annoyed with her for marrying him, and they never spoke to her afterwards, and that helped to break her heart, it did."

"Did she suffer very much?—was it a painful disease she died of at last?"

"No, mum, I can't say as it was, 'twas more like a sinking gradual like; and she were quite resigned, poor lady, and happy at last to go to a better world, she was. I never seed so peaceful a death, I didn't. I was well 'customed to see folks die, I was, for I have been nurse ever since my own husband died, more nor twenty-six years ago, and fearful sights I have seen."

"You did not live as nurse in one family, then—you were mostly employed to attend in illness, I suppose?"

"Oh! worse than that, mum. For four long years I was employed in Growfield Lunatic Asylum, and looking after the lunatics; and the frightful things I did see there, and the raving mad people, they a'most turned my brain, they did."

"At Growfield?" inquired Mrs. Dronington. "How many years ago was that?"

"It's nineteen years come next Michaelmas when I went there."

"Do you remember a patient called

Rachel Harraway?" inquired Mrs. Dronington, with eager curiosity.

"Rachel Harraway!—sure I do, indeed,"
said Mrs. Gwin, as the wild expression in
her eyes returned, and she became quite
agitated. "And it was she herself as drove
me most mad. The words she used to say
in her ravings come to my mind still, often
and often o' nights, and I hear the awful
tone of her voice, and that, as she imitated
the cry of a child."

"Tell me what she said, and about what
child—was it her own?"

"No, mum, I didn't think as how it was, I
do believe—I do think she had really burnt
some house, and took a light as was burning
on the table of a nursery somewhere, and set
fire to the cradle with the baby in it. Many
and many's the time she said all this and
more too; but I never like to think of it,
even after all these long years, only, mum,
you did seem so anxious to hear it, and so I
thought it better to tell it."

Mrs. Dronington's interest had been so strongly excited at finding that Mrs. Gwin knew Rachel Harraway, that for the moment she had almost forgotten her niece's illness, but after hearing some further details, she hurried the nurse into the adjoining room and installed her in her post by the bedside, resolving to question her still further the very next opportunity. After giving the prescribed medicine to her niece, and seeing that she was comfortably made up for the night, Mrs. Dronington went to bed.

CHAPTER XXXVI.

She is much frightened and puzzled.

MRS. Dronington lay awake for some time thinking of the unexpected coincidence, of the many coincidences that happen in life. The anxiety for her grand-daughter after she should become the wife of Sir Bevan, was sadly increased by what the old nurse told her,—and that anxiety kept her awake half the night. At last, wearied out by contending feelings, she was just sinking into a sound sleep when she heard a knock at her door, and her maid came in, saying that there was a telegram from Sir Charles Lillyford.

The poor old lady started up, rubbed her eyes, and having succeeded, after some difficulty, in putting on her spectacles, she read the following strange words:—"Your niece is very ill, and wishes to see you. We hope you will send without delay."

"What can they mean?—Wishes to see me! Why, ain't I always here with her? Sookey—do read this, and see if you can make head or tale of it?"

"Law, mum, I never was a good hand at reading writing, let alone being woke up out o' my sleep, and standing shivering in my bed-gown—and such a figure to have to appear before Mr. Spikehurst, and he in his night-cap, and worser than I; though my face is all tied up, for I have had such a bad toothache, and I had just dropt off to sleep—and forgot the pain."

"But it wants an answer, Sookey. Give me my desk, and I will try to write something," said Mrs. Dronington; "but I think they must be mad to send such a message as that, and by Telegram, too, in the middle of the night. 'Wishes to see you!'—they must mean 'us,' I suppose. Well, it was very kind of them to think of coming, to be sure; but—but let me see, what can I say? for, thank God, she is quite out of danger now. Here, Sookey, this pen will not write—try and find another—there on the writing-table. Have a care, now; don't put the candle so near the bed-curtains."

" Oh, mum, and I not so much as a flannel petticoat on, for surely I thought the house must be on fire at least—or Mrs. Lawrence took worse—and so I didn't wait to get a stitch o' clothes on."

" There, put on my shawl and dressing-gown, it's on the chair. I am so sorry you are cold. Let me see—now, what can I say? ' To Sir Charles Lillyford'—that is the way, I think—' my niece is out of danger, thank God.' Stay, the words are expensive," she said, putting her pen through the last words, "so one ought not to put more than is quite necessary;" and then began again on a fresh sheet of paper. " ' My niece is out of danger. Thanks—but you need not come.'

"I might leave out the 'thanks,' and it will be only ten, but I don't think that would look kind. There are only twelve words—that is even shorter than theirs was; I hope I made it plain, for Sir Charles must have put *you* instead of *us*, or not written the words plain. Is Mr. Spikehurst still there?"

"Oh! yes, mum, and gone to draw something to drink, and give the man which brought it, all the way from Muddleford Road Station, nine miles. It's pouring rain, it is, cats and dogs, I may say—a terrible night to be out, it is—which it's cold enough in the house, without even a flannel petticoat on."

"Then go and ask Spikehurst first to read this, and see if it's clear; for really my hand shakes so, with the alarm as to what the telegram might have been about, I am afraid I could not write it plain."

"Yes, I'll be sure and give it him, mum," said Sookey, as she put on one of Mrs. Dronington's shawls, and drew the folds over her head, to conceal the unbecoming head-gear as much as possible.

CHAPTER XXXVII.

Sir Bevan Desborough carries his point, but suffers from it.

" IL faut souffrir pour etre belle," says the old French proverb—referring, I suppose, to the manufactured article. And the same necessity applies to all efforts. The sufferings and the efforts have no particular limits; and the object is very apt to have a still longer range, keeping a little ahead, till the pursuit either tumbles into a quagmire, or turns back disappointed or weary. Certainly the pursuit of pleasure, as a final object, leads people over a path that is not strewn with roses; or if the roses are there, their petals are dead, and their thorns remain.

Sir Bevan was made practically aware of this truism as he walked through the lonely by-road in the pelting rain that night; (for Sir Bevan it was.) But there is no reason for supposing that it made him a "sadder and a wiser man;" on the contrary, the slight twinges of remorse which he felt while occupied in trying to humbug Fronica with a lame story about the scarlet fever having broken out at Langton Bridge, had acted as a stimulus instead of a warning.

It is true that she had had courage to speak to him, or write down before him, her opinion of his intended marriage, and of his cruelty towards her mother in the long years that had passed; and her speaking eyes, which reminded him painfully of his broken-hearted and forsaken wife, told him more than any words could do. But whatever impression they produced did not last, or result in more than his feeling that kind of shame which torments a cowardly nature with the fear of being found out.

When he left the cottage he slipped away by a footpath, and then crossing a meadow, reached the turnpike-road farther down. There he got into the hired carriage which had been waiting for him, and returned to London.

Had he been less cautious, and gone by the lane, he would actually have run over Mr. Sterndale, as he stood under the shadow of some firs, when the *onus probandi* would have rested with the latter; for what could be more natural than that Sir Bevan should go and visit his old nurse? But what was Mr. Sterndale doing there, at that time of night, waiting about with a dog-cart?

Sir Bevan arrived at his own house in Belgrave Square soon after midnight, went to bed immediately, and slept—yes, and soundly; whether through callousness or a sense of security, it would be difficult to determine. This state of comparatively happy oblivion would probably have lasted till his usual hour for waking up to the enjoyments or cares of his daily life ; but his rest, as well as that of poor Mrs. Dronington (whom we left struggling with the telegram in the last chapter), was doomed to be interrupted on that eventful night, or rather morning, for it was nearly eight o'clock when his valet knocked at the door, at first gently, but finding the sound produced no answer, and the case being urgent, he knocked so loud, that at last Sir Bevan called out, in no very amiable mood, to know why he was disturbed.

" Please, sir, it's a female, Mrs. Perkins, who is crying ready to break her heart, and says she must see you, sir, very particular."

" Mrs. Perkins !—what can she want ?" thought Sir Bevan, starting up from his pillow.

" I am sorry to disturb you, Sir Bevan," continued the valet, " but really she does take on so, I'm afraid something very dreadful has happened to somebody."

" Well, then, show her into the next

room, and I'll get up and see what it can be." "I suppose she's let that unfortunate girl escape," was the predominating thought while he dressed hurriedly, and went into the next room.

But it was far worse than this—at least, in poor Mrs. Perkins's opinion; and her agitation was so great, and her hysteric sobs and tears so violent, that for some minutes she was quite unable to explain what had occurred.

"Oh! dear, Sir Bevan, to think I should have lived to see this day! I am sure it warn't my fault, for I left everything quite safe, indeed I did. If I could give my right hand to save the poor girl's life, I'm sure I'd gladly do it, or hold it in the fire, I would, though it is most painful; and see, my arm has got dreadfully burnt in trying to save her."

"Burnt!—why, what has happened?—can't you tell me at once, instead of moaning and groaning there?"

"I will, indeed; but oh! dear, Sir Bevan, you ought to go away this very minute, and I came off at once, without anybody knowing where I went, to warn you. They will have it that you did it."

"Did what?—I believe you are going mad."

"Well, I am sure I have every reason to be so, from such a night, and all my china, and the best furniture, and the new beds— nothing was saved!"

"What! do you mean that the house was on fire?"

"Yes, and it must have broke out not ten minutes after you drove away, 'cause John Bowles says he could swear it was you, and he see the carriage driving as fast as ever the horses could carry it by Turner's Pond, and down the hill by the lime-kiln, and John Blann see'd the same."

"Do you mean to say that poor girl was burnt?" inquired Sir Bevan, in a loud tone. "Why did you not save her?"

"It was quite impossible, for the walls was all wainscote, and great old beams all across the ceiling, and it burnt with such awful fury."

"Where were you when it burst out? I suppose you had not returned from your sister's?"

"No, sir, I had not; and of course I'm nigh crazed, for t'was my fault for not being in the house, 'cause I suppose that the fire caught——"

"And she was locked into her room!—my God forgive me!" said Sir Bevan, in a hoarse voice.

"T'was both our faults, Sir Bevan, for I ought not to have given in to your plan about that poor helpless girl, who could not even scream out for help when the flames was burning under her feet."

Sir Bevan covered his face with his hands, for the image of Fronica's countenance as he had so lately seen it, rose up in fearful distinctness before him; and the likeness to her mother, the only woman he had ever really loved, became more apparent to Memory's eye.

Both were silent for a few minutes, and then Mrs. Perkins said,

"Oh! I do—I do believe it's a warning, for that poor girl's eyes did seem to speak to me plainer than any tongue ever did, and they made me feel more like a sinner as I am, than I ever did before. And, oh! sir, what could you have been going to do with her, for sure such a saint-like look as she had, as if she was too good for this world?"

"I meant her no harm—I tell you I did not."

"I know you did not, or I don't think I ever would have consented to lock the door upon her that way. But now I see the time is going on, and I do fear they'll come and take you, sir, for there is going to be a inquest as soon as they could find the poor girl's body."

Sir Bevan shuddered, and at that moment he thought he would have given up Beatrice herself if he could recall that child—his child—to life!

"Why could no one get a ladder?" he said, "and try to save her?—and why did no one come till the whole house was burnt?"

"Yes, Sir Bevan, numbers of neighbours went there," said Mrs. Perkins; "but you know, sir, it was half a mile from the village, and by the time we all got there, the flames was raging from the bottom up to the very top story—they was coming out of the very windows of the room she was in, so there was no chance for her; and by the time the engine came from Barford, there was nothing but the bare walls. Oh! my God! such a fearful sight it was—the night so dark, and the flames crackled and roared, and then the roof fell in, and we all knew that no living thing could be left within that blazing furnace. But, Sir Bevan, do mind about yourself now, because there is a-many gossiping people there, and I heard one or two of them a-saying it was you did it. Now, in course every one knows you wouldn't; but when people gets a-talking in that way, it may make great unpleasantness."

Sir Bevan felt the full force of the advice, for if anyone saw him coming out of the cottage alone, it might look very ugly; and, at any rate, the mere report, if it got about, coupled with the other rumours which he knew were in circulation against him, and the known disappearance of Fronica, might —there was no saying what it might *not* do, or undo for him. Perhaps, for the first time in his life, he knew what it was to experience mental suffering; nor was it solely caused by the fear of social loss. The dreadful death of his own child, by his own fault, the long tale of wrongs done in cold blood over a period of eighteen years to her and her mother, rose up suddenly before him then, with a vividness that made them seem new, and for a few moments he shivered with remorse like one in an ague fit.

But the deep-rooted habits of a life are stronger than pangs of remorse, when the latter proceed from regret rather than from repentance; and Sir Bevan soon found himself reasoning as follows :—

"The only way to silence that sort of thing is to have no delay about the marriage, for if there is any delay people will begin to talk, and then I shall have a whole pack of them down upon me. The wedding must be to-day instead of to-morrow. Another letter from my sister at Nice—worse—not expected to recover. Rather a lame story, that—but it must do. These people, whoever they may be (I wish they were at the bottom of the sea), are ferreting out my concerns, as I learnt in Fronica's note, for the sake of Beatrice; and by the same token they will leave them alone for her sake, as soon as she is married. Miss Gubbings will be the spoke in that wheel; for she can't marry Roland Lillyford till his debts are paid, and she won't stick Sir Charles to insisting on the engagement without. Luckily I have got a special licence, so it won't signify about being after twelve o'clock. I must go to the City at once, and settle about the money being paid for Roland; and then to Portman Square—there isn't a moment to be lost—it's nearly nine o'clock now."

He took one or two rapid turns up and down the room, too much absorbed to notice Mrs. Perkins, who all this time had continued to sob and lament.

At last, however, it occurred to him that her presence in his own particular sitting-room was an extra annoyance, and that his first step must be to dismiss her; so he said, as kindly as he could,

" Well, Mary, don't cry any more, it can't be helped, you didn't mean to do anything neglectful; you had better return at once to Langton Bridge, and see what can be done, and you know you may depend upon my assistance. I am very busy now—I must be off to see my lawyer directly. Good-bye."

"Yes, sir, I'll go . . . I know, sir, you be going to be married to-morrow, and, Sir Bevan, indeed I hopes you'll be happy, which there's nobody, I'll make bold to say, after the mother that bore you, is fonder of you than your old nurse; and you are been very good to me, and never let me want for nothing; and often and often's the time when I think of you as you was when you was a boy, and how proud my lady and Sir George was of you, and spoilt you, that she did, poor lady, when your father died, and there was nobody but me to put on the first pair of breeches you ever had, which I remember was blue, with gilt buttons, and how he did kick and bite with feeling hisself so uncomfortable, bless his little heart, I've got the mark of your teeth in my arm now, Sir Bevan, that I have. But I be keeping of you, and you wants to be getting along. And I hopes you go over to France at once, sir, till this 'quest is over, and sich like. Good day, sir."

So saying, she took Sir Bevan's hand, raised it to her lips, then dropped a curtsy and walked out of the room.

A few minutes afterwards Sir Bevan was on his way to the City.

LONDON: UBE.